CATH HOWE

ALSO AVAILABLE BY

CATH HOWE:

ELLA on the OUTSIDE

×

Not MY Fault

×

HOW to be ME

CATH HOWE

nosy
crow

To my parents, D and D

C. H.

xxx

First published in the UK in 2022 by Nosy Crow Ltd
The Crow's Nest, 14 Baden Place,
Crosby Row, London SE1 1YW

Nosy Crow Eireann Ltd
44 Orchard Grove, Kenmare
Co Kerry V93 FY22, Ireland

ISBN: 9781788006125

A CIP catalogue record for this book is available from the British Library

Printed and bound in Great Britain by Clays Ltd, Elcograf S.p.A.
Typeset by Tiger Media

Papers used by Nosy Crow are made from wood grown in sustainable forests.

3 5 7 9 10 8 6 4 2

www.nosycrow.com

Chapter 1
Callie

I used to think I knew my friends so well. But now I think friends are mysterious icebergs. There's so much going on under the surface.

Friends are like the family you choose. I read that on a birthday card. I don't need a bigger family, that's for sure; there's six of us. I did sort of choose my friend Ted. We've been together since nursery. We always sat next to each other and sang and played with the bricks. He's small and very quiet and he hates speaking in class. He won't ever answer a question unless the teacher says his name, and we all wait for him to open his mouth. Mostly, he's just quiet. We don't need everyone to be noisy, do we? Ted's like a cat appearing beside you, watching. You wonder what he's thinking.

Recently he's got even quieter. I often sit beside him for a chat on the planter at lunchtime, looking out over the football game, but these days it's mostly me chatting and him listening with that concentrating expression he has.

I wonder if part of the reason he got sadder was because he stopped coming round to my house after school each day. He had been coming to us for years. But this term his mum rang and cancelled it.

Also, a few weeks ago, a big thing happened to make Ted feel much worse.

We were planning our class assembly and we were told we had to read out a letter pretending to be a soldier writing to his family from the trenches in World War One.

Ted didn't want to do it. Every time we practised, Mr Dunlop shouted at him, "Can't hear you!" and "We'll have no wimping out in my class."

Ted flushed and his voice came out smaller and smaller until it was a whisper. I wanted to help him improve but, even though he lives next door, we don't usually see each other outside of school now. I had loads of netball sessions ready for a big competition too, so I was very busy, but I did try to give Ted some tips during playtimes. We practised being louder and not looking right at the audience but at a place above their heads. But he really didn't get any better.

"I just wish someone else could read it out," he kept saying. So the whole class knew how wound up he was.

On the big day, five minutes before our assembly started, a whole group of kids from my class were messing about, chasing each other with water bottles because our teacher had gone out of the room. Just as we were about to file into the hall, a boy called Billy Feldon squirted a carton of orange juice down the front of Ted's trousers. Ted didn't notice. Not at the time. I certainly didn't or I would have told him. Especially because of what happened next.

We lined up and walked silently down the stairs into the hall, all the way to the front. The whole school was in there. We all filed along and turned to face the audience. That's when everyone saw the dark wet patch right across the front of Ted's trousers. He looked down at that exact same moment and did a kind of terrible gasping face. So of course we all thought Ted had wet himself, because of being so nervous. It was terrible because Miss James called out, "Ted, love, let's sort you out," and Ted had to come out of the line and walk back out of the hall in front of the whole entire world!

After that, Ted wouldn't talk to anyone. His mum went to see the head teacher and THE TRUTH CAME OUT about Billy and the orange juice because some people had seen what Billy did. We all discussed whether Billy would get suspended. But I don't think squirting orange juice was bad enough, especially as Billy just kept saying the squirting had been an accident.

My friend Ted seemed different after that. I heard a couple of kids calling him Toilet Ted one break time. School can be mean.

Chapter 2
Ted

I wasn't always a night visitor.

High up in the tree in my garden, inside the clustering leaves, I looked down on Callie's garden next door.

If I concentrated, Callie felt nearer.

Everything in my head crowded into remembering one thing: that day, a long time ago, when we were playing in her garden and a friend of Callie's mum's had pointed to me and asked Callie, "Is this one of your brothers?" And she had smiled with her whole face and said, "No, Ted's my nearly-brother."

I felt warm through and through.

That's what I was: a nearly-brother.

But I ruined it. I made a mistake, just after term started two months ago.

Mum and I had just come back from the doctor's for my height and weight check.

I remember Dr Lowell's questions.

"Well now, how does he eat?"

With a knife and fork, you weirdo! I thought.

"He's fine, Dr Lowell," Mum said. "He's got a good appetite."

Why didn't he ask me?

"Ted's below average for height but he's still

within the range." The doctor pointed to a chart with coloured columns and percentages. "He's here, at the lower end. We might do a few blood tests, just to be on the safe side. Ask at the desk and the nurse will sort you out."

"Well now, sweetheart," the nurse said when we got there. "What can I do for you?"

She didn't call Mum "sweetheart"! That's what gets me: the sort of words people use when they talk to me. "Poppet". "Honey". That voice. Patting me. People always think I'm younger inside my head as well as being small.

Sometimes, though, I wonder what would happen if I never got any bigger. Would they keep me at school forever? No one would ever take me seriously. I dreamed once that they took me back into the infants. We think you would be happier in here.

On the way back from the doctor's, we stopped at the supermarket. When we got home, Mum looked at the receipt for the shopping and sighed. "We're going to have to cut some corners. Money's tight."

Mum is a bookkeeper. She does accounts for local businesses. She's always working, but everything's getting more expensive. And she had just had to pay a big bill for our heating to be mended.

Just like that, I said, "I don't need to be childminded at Callie's every day after school. That would save us some money."

Mum stopped putting away the shopping. "I thought you loved going to Callie's?"

Then, instead of saying, "Yeah, I do," I said, "Plenty of people in my year walk home on their own and let themselves in."

Mum nodded. "That's true."

"I've got a key."

"Course you have." Mum looked pleased now. "Great. I'll ring and sort it."

It was waiting on my tongue to say, "Don't!" I just had to speak. But I didn't.

I know why. I suppose I was fed up of people thinking I was a little scrappy kid. I didn't need to go to Callie's and stay for tea and play in her garden with the other kids until Mum got back. But I did want to. Just – in that moment, in that split second, I forgot how much.

But now, as I realised that part of my life would be gone, a huge lump arrived in my throat.

I watched Mum pick up her phone and call Callie's mum. We were going to make our own arrangements from now on, she said, smiling over at me. "Here's a week's notice."

It was like the door of Callie's house had firmly closed in my face.

I would be a visitor now. And it was my fault!

Chapter 3

Callie

Half term came and went, and on the first Monday back we had another assembly and in this one they told us they were choosing new prefects. Prefects were like super pupils, I always thought, when I was in the infants. And today our teachers made a massive fuss about how important prefects were, saying it was a special job. If a visitor came to the school a prefect could show them round, or they could get the hall ready for assemblies, or maybe do the sound from the laptop, sitting on a chair at the back. Prefects set an example, they said, and we all sat up straighter, as if someone had pushed a pole down our backs.

When we went out to play afterwards, my friend Zara said, "Would we miss lots of lessons if we're prefects?" because Zara hates missing anything.

Nico said, "Who cares if we miss stuff?"

I secretly thought I had a good chance of being chosen because I was in the netball team and not usually late for school, even if I did have to run some mornings. I only live round the corner but that makes it worse, I think, because I don't leave enough time to get to school, like I'm expecting to fly there. My garden backs on to the playground, so I can hear people arriving and games of football while I'm frantically trying to find things in the kitchen with the minutes ticking down until I'm officially late. But I always make it, dropping stuff, still pulling my coat on, legging it up the road and tumbling into the crowds by the gates.

Nico is the tallest person in our class. "I can look over things," he told us. "That might be useful for being a prefect."

Well, I wasn't going to get picked for height. And Ted is the smallest in our class so that wasn't very kind of Nico with Ted standing right beside him. Ted just looked a bit bleak and shrugged.

"My dad always says, 'They don't make diamonds as big as bricks'," I told them. Nico chased me round the back of the planter for that.

Zara said, "Height would be a stupid way to decide. Imagine if the teachers decided who was going to be head teacher by lining up and picking the tallest!"

We all suggested teachers who we thought were tall but then we realised the tallest adult in school was Mr Rafferty, the caretaker. We laughed a lot then.

I didn't set a bad example at school. Not like

Billy Feldon who, worse luck, was next to me in the register, so he was always beside me in class. If you had to pick someone to sit next to, you would never pick Billy because: he never sits still, he never has the stuff he's supposed to bring and he's just … irritating. He messes around, not in a loud way but like a buzzing fly on a window – you always know he's there. He borrows my things, he hasn't brought colouring pencils or he's lost the worksheet we were given. At parents' evening, Mum complained that I always got put next to Billy, and our teacher said, "Callie is a sensible girl." That sounds really boring, but I wouldn't want to be like Billy, chasing his tail, trying to find something he forgot. He's always nudging me. "Callie, what did he say?" or "Callie, let's both use your answer sheet." He doesn't even ask nicely!

He's kind of stupid-silly. He says things like, "What's an Ig?"

"Don't know…"

"An Eskimo's house without a loo." Then he cracks up laughing.

He's obsessed with choices: "Hey, Callie, feet for ears or ears for feet?" poking me with a ruler. "Callie, Callie, listen. Would you rather be eaten from the inside quickly or from the outside slowly?"

On and on.

His jokes aren't funny. And anyway, you shouldn't laugh at your own jokes. We tried to stop laughing at Billy's after what he did to Ted in assembly.

Billy Feldon has all these theories about our teacher Mr Dunlop. He says Mr Dunlop is secretly a troll. Billy says classic troll behaviour under his breath whenever Mr Dunlop does something we don't like. Mr Dunlop is one of those teachers who tells us off a lot so that we all feel a bit flat. He's always disappointed. He's got this miserable voice and he does long sighs. Billy copies them. A typical day would be:

1. Mr Dunlop telling us off about people fighting over whose turn it is to have the football

2. A general telling-off about behaviour, and then:

3. Threats about losing play times and all kinds of horrible punishments that might happen to us.

Billy will be rolling his eyes, copying Mr Dunlop and sighing, whispering, "Classic troll behaviour" in the same low voice. Other classic troll behaviour is a throat-clearing thing that Mr Dunlop does. Billy says that's because trolls eat disgusting things and they don't chew properly so there are always bits stuck in their throats.

There's a window next to Billy and he's always leaning up against it and rattling the metal arm, making a grating, scraping noise, pressing down and working it loose. Mr Dunlop looks around, trying to work out where the noise is coming from. Billy whispers under his breath, "The trolls are coming." It makes us happy that Mr Dunlop doesn't know. It makes us feel that anything might happen.

We don't want to help Mr Dunlop because he doesn't want to help us. If we were younger, someone would put their hand up and say, "Please, Mr Dunlop, the noise is coming from that window over there."

But these days my class just enjoy watching our teacher get cross.

x

We are unusual in my school, being a four. Zara, Nico, Ted and me. It's because they chose us four for maths masterclasses more than a year ago.

Every Wednesday for two hours, the four of us get taken round to Larks Cross, the secondary school next door, for extra maths. There are lots of children from other schools there too, but we always sit in our small group and share our answers to the fiendish reasoning questions. We discovered that Zara was the fastest of all of us. It wasn't a surprise; she's super serious and she always gets her homework in on time. Nico was the loudest. And if he thinks he knows the answer he will never change it, even when you have shown him why it's wrong. Ted hardly speaks, but he has an amazing memory. I like going to Larks Cross because that's where we'll go next year and anyway my brother Elliot already goes there so I can look out for him on his way to lessons with his friends. If he's going past our room, he always does something like jumping high and waving, to make sure I see him.

Chapter 4
Callie

In the afternoon, they read out the names of the new prefects. We all got excited and tried not to show it. I was sure Zara would get picked. I had my fingers crossed under the table. And then … they didn't pick me or any of my friends.

When Mr Dunlop called out six names, the last one was … Billy!

Billy did this double blink beside me, bolt upright, mouth open. "Me?"

"You?" I said.

I couldn't believe it and neither could the others. Outside in the crowded playground, Nico was fuming. "I feel as if I've been kicked in the head by a horse. Billy Feldon, he's a disaster on legs!"

"He doesn't ever get to school on time!" Zara said. "So unfair!"

"That's not the worst thing," Ted said, his face like thunder. "He shouldn't be in our school."

"Sorry," we all said. "Sorry, Ted."

"I think we should go on strike," Nico said. "Refuse to sit down in assembly."

Zara nodded. "We should write to our Member of Parliament. Hold a sit-in."

We found Miss Reynolds on playground duty

by the drinking fountain. We all like Miss Reynolds cos she runs lots of cross-country events and she celebrates if you try to do something, even if you're rubbish.

"Sometimes a prefect learns to set a better example," she said, "by being made one."

"What about us then?" we demanded.

"There will be more prefect roles later in the year. The best thing you can do is to volunteer for things," she said. "Like the Maths Challenge, for example. You are an obvious team for that. I'll put you down." She grinned. "There's lots of ways you could be helpful too – how about classroom monitor jobs? If you help, the teachers will remember it next time they're choosing more prefects."

Then she got called away to deal with a bang on the head incident.

"Hang on, did Miss Reynolds just volunteer us for the Maths Challenge?" Nico muttered. "Why did we bother to ask her?"

"I don't mind doing the Maths Challenge," Zara said. "We could practise. It'll be fun."

Nico was still fuming. "I'll do the maths thing, but I am not sharpening pencils and sucking up to teachers! No thanks."

I wasn't very interested in sharpening things or trying to find all the missing scissors either.

"If Billy's a rubbish prefect, could he get de-prefected?" I asked.

"Dunno," everyone said.

I sat on the planter with Ted in afternoon play, watching the football.

"How could they make Billy a prefect? It doesn't make sense," I said. "They don't know what he's like."

"Dunlop does," Ted said softly.

"I don't think Dunlop really knows what any of us is like."

Ted looked so fed up.

"Maybe he'll just be rubbish. I bet he will be," I said.

Ted swung his legs. "So why choose him? He doesn't care about people."

We stopped chatting to watch a builder in a high-vis jacket cross the playground and disappear behind the tarpaulin near the gates. There's a lot going on in our school at the moment. They are adding a class to each year in the juniors so there will be three classes instead of two. Before the holidays started, they all came tramping in past the hall in hard hats with bright yellow jackets. They did an assembly on how to build new bits of a school, showing us the plans for the new classrooms. That was OK, but we've got used to them so it's not so exciting any more.

They were supposed to finish in the summer holidays but they still hadn't, so we had to listen to them banging and drilling. The inside walls were bare down at that end of school, and there were plastic covers on all the carpets. Outside, the building work was screened off by a tarpaulin like a great big blue sheet around the outside, so there was nothing to see. We were banned from going anywhere near it. When I went for maths masterclasses we could look down and see the new classrooms from Larks Cross. They just looked the same as all the other classrooms except they didn't have windows yet; four rectangular boxes, two on top of two, and ladders and pulleys and planks and builders up on the scaffolding.

Chapter 5
Callie

Later on that day, we burst out of school as usual. Most of us walk home on our own. The teachers have a list of who's allowed to.

We set off. Nico and Zara come home with me every day and their parents collect them later because my mum is their childminder.

Ted walked with us then waved when we got to his house. He had his key ready in his hand. "Bye!"

It's always noisy at home because there's soooo many of us. There's my brother Ollie and little sister Chloe, and two other little ones, Timmy and Benjy, who Mum collects from our school nursery at lunchtime. There's my older brother, Elliot, but he is often out. And with Nico and Zara, that makes eight of us. My sister and brother argue a lot. When everyone shouts, we are a major headache, Mum says.

Zara and Nico and me are a bit like grown-ups in my house, even though we're not. Mum calls us my sensible big ones. But this means if we hang around after tea, even for a few seconds, Mum makes us stack the dishwasher and wipe faces and tables. It's so boring! The best thing is to say we've got schoolwork to do and disappear down to the summerhouse at the end of the garden, just to get away from all the screaming and arguments.

Today we watched TV when we got home and moaned to Mum about the prefect thing. We were all feeling raw about it.

My mum's a good listener. "See how things go," she said. "Maybe they're trying to encourage some of the naughty ones by giving them more things to do."

When tea was over we did our usual thing, stacking the dirty plates and helping with the little ones, then asking to get down. By six thirty it was getting dark. Zara's dad and Nico's mum always collected them some time after half past seven.

"Can we do some homework in the summerhouse, Mum?"

Mum smiled and leaned against a kitchen chair. "Course you can."

We all leaped up.

I caught the words, "Put your coats on!" as we slammed the kitchen door.

We're lucky to have the summerhouse. It has lights, a bashed old sofa and beanbags and cushions. When it's cold, we can put the heater on.

Nico ran down to the end of my garden where there's a tyre hanging from the cherry tree. It's not a massive tree, not like the one at the end of Ted's garden next door, but it's sturdy. You can see the marks in the trunk from where the rope has cut into it. Nico leapt on and swung. He always tries to whack the branch above, and the side of the tree, bending, pulling hard and swinging violently. He gets up speed and really goes for it.

I watched him for a moment then pushed through the long grass near the fence, skirting round the nettles.

Over the fence, if you stand on tiptoes, you can see our school laid out behind the trees and, on your left, the playground apparatus with its mini climbing wall and monkey bars.

I noticed something near me and jumped in shock: past the brambles and straggly weeds there was a large hole as wide as a kitchen chair, right up close to our fence. It looked as if someone was digging their way out of the garden.

"Hey, you two, come and look!" I called.

They both came over.

"Keep back, you'll fall down it," Zara said.

Nico studied the hole. "Seriously impressive," he said.

"What would make a hole like that? A cat?" I asked.

Nico pushed through the weeds and jumped down inside it. "It goes right underneath," he called. His voice went muffled as he twisted round and disappeared. Then he popped back up again. His eyes shone. "It comes up in the playground!"

"That's … not very exciting," I said.

Zara stared at the hole. "I don't like it. Why would anyone…?"

Nico grinned up at us. "You're wrong. It's fun." He dived back down again and disappeared, calling, "Come on. Last one inside the playground's a loser!"

Chapter 6
Ted

Once you're back from school every day, stay at home, Mum said. I need to know where you are.

From the top of the tree, I watched my friends swing on the tyre where I used to swing, and stared inside the summerhouse, with its bright-coloured cushions where we all used to lie around after school, chatting and playing games. I remembered the kitchen at Callie's, and the calling and shouting and everyone pouncing on the food.

My house felt silent and cold every day.

They couldn't see me in the tree. They never looked up here anyway.

x

The next thing to go wrong was our class assembly. A letter from the trenches in World War One.

Callie had said she would help me practise but we never got much time.

My voice came out small and squeaky in the huge echoey hall during our class rehearsal. "Dear Mum and Dad..."

"Louder!" shouted Mr Dunlop.

"Dear Mum and Dad. Life in the trenches is very hard and the food is bad..."

"Can't hear you."

No one would ever hear me. I thought of all the parents at the back filming us. I would ruin it.

"Could someone else read it?" I asked.

"You wrote it, lad, you're gonna read it," Mr Dunlop snapped.

"My leg..." I began.

Someone giggled behind me.

"Fell off!" murmured Billy Feldon.

Laughs rippled around the class. Lots of people were shuffling about and fidgeting now.

I felt the hot flush in my cheeks. I tried again. "My leg—"

"Grew wings and flew in a tree!" Billy said, just loud enough for everyone on the benches behind me to hear. There was a huge burst of laughter.

Someone made the noise of a flying leg. Whee pdung.

Mr Dunlop's mouth went tight. "I don't want to hear a single other voice. Some of you are going to be in detention all week at this rate."

Everyone went quiet.

"And as for you, Ted, come right out in front. Chin up. Big voice."

But my voice had shrunk to a shrew's. "Dear Mum and Dad."

Mr Dunlop's face was red and cross. "These soldiers, they were brave. What does 'brave' mean, Ted?"

Everyone waited.

It means attacking enemies, I thought. But I didn't say anything.

Mr Dunlop sighed. "How about you try being brave, just for once?"

I was useless at being brave. If people in our year jostle you by the lockers, I pretty much got smashed against them because they were bigger and heavier than me. There was nothing I could do. They pretended it was an accident. One time I ended up actually stranded on top of the lockers and Mr Dunlop shouted at me to get down when in fact I'd ended up there in a massive crowd bundle outside the classroom. Someone had hauled me on their shoulders and I ended up clinging there.

Now when someone does something and the air goes prickly, ready for fights to start, I pretend I forgot something important and rush away as if I need to collect something. Just to be anywhere else.

So I wasn't brave. Mr Dunlop was right.

And then the assembly. I have to say about our assembly. Billy Feldon squirted me with orange juice, except I didn't know. By the time everyone saw the front of my trousers they all thought I'd wet myself, thanks to Billy. Now I was the class joke even more than before.

The day after our assembly we had a cover teacher. He called out my name in the register and when I said good morning, he said, "Oh, there's a note here in the register about you." And he read out to the class, "Please allow Ted to go to the toilet whenever he asks and offer him the chance whenever you can." He nodded and smiled at me. "You only have to ask."

Gales of laughter came after that. The cover teacher said, "Oh, sorry, I don't think I was supposed to read that out."

I don't know who wrote that note. I think it was Billy. He laughed loudest.

I didn't want to be Ted any more. I would be someone else. Someone … better.

Now, crouched high up in the branches of the tree, I watched as Callie and the others found the hole under her fence. Of course. It had been there for days.

I was the night visitor. Time to watch what they did next.

Chapter 7
Callie

We weren't allowed in our school playground at night. This was sending a thrill through me.

It wasn't completely dark; the sky was grey, like a big sheet of metal, with clouds like silvery broccoli and a huge moon. The lamps on the tops of the scaffolding on the other side of the playground glowed like street lights and lit up the tarpaulin wrapped round the new classrooms.

We wandered around the village of little cabins in the trees. We chased each other and jumped out. It felt so different from daytime; risky ... mysterious.

We didn't usually come here. During the day some younger kids finished their lunch at top speed just to get out here first and sit inside the cabins or play hide-and-seek among the trees. Now it was all ours.

Nico leapt out at me from behind one of the little cabins. "Boo!"

Zara made a noise and we all giggled.

"What shall we do now?" Nico asked.

"I'm not sure," Zara said.

"Scaredy cat!"

"Be quick," I said.

Back at home, Timmy and Benjy would be collected soon and Mum would give my brother and sister a bath. Mum is a punctual and exact person. We are allowed to play in the garden until seven thirty. Ollie and Chloe have ten minutes in a bath and then they are back downstairs. That's the time we come back up the garden, fling open the kitchen door and find my friends' coats and bags before pick-up.

"Race you to the apparatus," I called. "Come on; the moon's behind the clouds, we just have to go quick."

We ran to the apparatus. I climbed up the net until I was giggling and tangled. You could never hang here during the day because someone would complain to the playground supervisor and say it was their turn.

We should get back home. I pictured Mum chasing Ollie and Chloe with a towel and bundling them up, saying, "Snug as a bug in a rug," and sending them to find pyjamas.

We ran over to the water fountain right by our classroom windows. I could see my table from here, and the window where Billy was always fiddling with the catch. I gave the frame the tiniest nudge. The window dropped open.

"No way! It's opened," Nico whispered.

"It's always loose," I said, nudging it shut.

Nico giggled. "They could have burglars!"

That made giggles spurt up inside all of us.

But then suddenly a light came on inside school at the far end, by the library.

"Someone's in there!" Zara hissed.

Chapter 8
Billy

I shouldn't have switched the desk lamp on.

It was nice having a proper light, though.

It was going to be great sleeping at school. It was a laugh. An adventure. It was my secret clever thing.

Anyway, there wasn't anywhere else!

I padded around the library in my socks.

A school was a bit like a hotel, really: long corridors, people coming to visit for a while, free Wi-Fi and TV, hot drinks in some of the rooms.

I'd pretend the food here was the best food in the world; I could have all the staffroom cereals in one bowl if I wanted. No more Moor Lane School. I decided I would rename it Reina Vittoria, which means Queen Victoria. That was where Mum was now; the Reina Vittoria Hotel in Lanzarote. She would be on a sun lounger next to the pool. So she was in her hotel and I was in mine. Fun. Definitely fun. And short; only a week. A week is nothing, is it? Piece of cake. Ha ha!

The plan had been for me to stay at Dad's while Mum was away. She booked the holiday with her friend Stella and spent ages sorting out things I'd need, like breakfast and school uniform. She would never have left if she'd known I was now dragging beanbags into a sleeping pile in the school library. She would have a fit. She would jump back on to the plane and fly home to rescue me with that furious look on her face. You and me, Billy. Us against the world.

Dad had agreed I could stay at his house. He was even supposed to be having some time off work so we could spend some afternoons together. But Dad only cared about his new family now. He didn't think about Mum and me.

He changed the plan, didn't he? Mum left for the holiday and the first night at Dad's was OK, because I stayed in K's room while she was at a friend's sleepover. But on Sunday evening she came back. It was THE NIGHT OF HORRORS. All because of K. I'm not going to use her name. But I was lucky to survive, seriously! And that was with Dad in the house! So now, imagine Monday morning when he told me he had to be away for the rest of the week for work. "Look, mate, what with the new baby I just have to take every job," he said. "Do you understand? Normally wild horses wouldn't have dragged me away."

Yeah, right.

I knew then, I couldn't sleep there another

night. It would be the end of me.

I did ask Sami if I could stay at his nan's house but he said no, not since we got in trouble; she never wants to see me again, basically. We borrowed her food mixer to make slime and then we fought over it and Sami says I smashed it. I think it was half and half.

For a while, I was stuck for ideas. I spent the whole of Monday in school with my brain coiling and broiling. Where could I sleep for one week – bed and breakfast, comfortable accommodation? I couldn't go home because our neighbour Vicky was keeping an eye on our flat and she would tell Mum if she saw me. And then Mum would get on a plane and come home. And then Mum and Dad would have a big row and Mum wouldn't get her holiday. Mum had to have her holiday. Mum's an intensive-care nurse and she was really tired.

All through maths, geography and PE on Monday, ideas went round and round in my head and I ended up with one big idea that was my best yet. A brilliant plan. Stay in school for the week.

I'd been doing parent tours – people in the area who want to see round the school because they might choose it for their kid. I'd walked right round every bit of school, even near where the builders were working, past the hall and the music practice rooms and the nursery. School was OK. I was used to school. I wouldn't tell Mum. I could just send messages. She would never know.

And I had a bit of money that Mum had given me for emergencies.

My teacher, Mr Dunlop, is always saying we should use our initiative. So I used mine.

It was a good thing I had been made a prefect; it meant I could ask questions and people wouldn't say go back to your classroom and stop asking stupid questions, you irritating child.

So I started making my plan. At lunchtime I went hunting for our caretaker, Mr Rafferty.

He has a little workroom office next to the library. I peered through the glass door. There were piles of tools and wires and cardboard boxes on a little low table and the walls had little grippers with even more tools and equipment. It was like Aladdin's Cave.

Mr Rafferty opened the door a crack. He rubbed his beard. "What is it?"

"Mr Rafferty," I said. "My class is doing a survey

about school to help prefects show people round. Can I ask you some questions?"

He muttered something, locked up his room and plunged the key into his overalls. "You'll have to be quick, lad," he said gruffly.

"Shall I help you?" I asked.

Mr Rafferty is always sort of friendly-grumpy, so I just smiled and walked beside him to the small hall. "School council meeting," he muttered. "Chairs out."

I collected a chair from the stack in the corridor, opened it out and put it beside his.

"Do you go in every room at the end of the day?" I asked.

"What on earth's that got to do with showing people round?"

"Background information," I said.

He grunted. "I check thc whole place. Can't risk something being left switched on by mistake. Or a window being left open."

"That's very useful," I said.

He grunted again and spun two chairs above his head then put them down.

"Do you live in our school?" I asked.

"Live here? No! No one lives here!"

"Good – I mean, OK. Do you lock up every night at the same time?"

"Nope. The time varies." I think he was enjoying explaining. "The main hall could be hired out for a parent event or a local church. But normally I close up about six thirty. Mrs Alexander will often still be in a meeting right up until I do my rounds. In the mornings, I'm in at half past seven."

"That's incredibly interesting," I said. "Do the lights still come on at night?"

"They're on a sensor. They won't stay on. Movement triggers them." He shook his head. "Why are you asking that?"

"I just love … electrical things," I said. "Shall I put out more chairs?"

"That'll do," he said.

I would make a good spy. I said thank you. I like Mr Rafferty.

After school I went straight back to Dad's. Patti opened the door with her shirt not done up properly and a towel over one shoulder with the baby on it. The baby was making little squawks.

"I'm not going to be staying here this week after all," I told her. "I'm at a friend's."

"Oh!" Patti sighed and nudged the baby further

up on her shoulder. "You'd better come in. I can't leave this door open."

I went in and collected my overnight bag from the hallway. "The friend is in my class. We're doing a project. It's better if I stay at her house. We can work on it," I said.

"Great." The baby made a mewing noise and threw up on Patti's shoulder. She said something rude and pushed a white cloth under its head. I panicked in case she asked me to hold it. No one's actually asked me to hold that baby. There are photos of K on the mantelpiece, scowling, with the baby on her knee.

Thinking about K made me shudder and I swung my bag up over my shoulder. "I'll go now."

The baby started to scream. Patti said a swear word. "All right then. Have fun. I'm sure your dad will call you."

Easy! My plan was falling into place.

Chapter 9
Billy

Next, off to the chip shop to buy my dinner. I love fish and chips. Dad used to buy me fish and chips sometimes when we were walking back after an evening football game. I sat on a swing at the rec, where my junior league football training happens on a Saturday morning. Staring across the field and thinking about Dad made me feel a bit rubbish, to be honest, but I could balance the packet of food across my knees and no one would disturb me, now that all the little kids had gone home for tea.

I watched some pigeons pecking around my feet and threw one a chip.

Dad didn't tell Mum about Patti; we didn't know anything about her. The way Mum and Dad shouted all the time just seemed normal, and then one day in the summer holidays I found Dad packing a case while Mum was out shopping. It was a big case. He was emptying drawers into it.

"What are you doing, Dad?"

Dad leapt like a burglar.

"Just ... grabbing some things I'll need for a few days," he said.

Why didn't he look at me?

"Is it for a holiday?" I asked.

He winced. "No."

"So why then?"

"Look, Billy, I just need to go now." He held up a sweatshirt and squashed it in the case.

"Can I come too?"

His face wobbled. He pursed his lips. "Maybe," he said. "When I've got things straight..."

"But where are you going?"

He grabbed a coat off the back of the door. "I can't do this," he said. I reached out to hug him and he held me at arm's length, like I was dangerous. "I really have to go," he said. "You'll still be my best boy."

He threw on his leather jacket and rushed down the path with the case. The gate clanged, then there was just the empty space.

I must have known to go in his room and find him packing. If I hadn't, I would have thought he'd just ... disappeared.

You'll still be my best boy. The words stung me. I kept finding them in my head. You'll still be my best boy.

When Mum got back, I said Dad had packed a case and she said, "He'll have to tell you himself. I'm not doing it. Now, let's sort out this shopping."

She wouldn't talk about it at all.

A week later Dad turned up on the touchline at my football training and bought me a bun and a drink afterwards. He said, "Mate, there's someone I need to tell you about..." And I realised that when my dad is going to say the worst things, he always starts by calling me mate.

"I've got this friend," he said.

"Does Mum know?"

"Yes, yes, of course."

"Aren't you going to live with us any more?"

"You'll still see me, Billy, just ... not so often."

That was three months ago. Since then I've hardly seen him at all. Mum always catches up on sleep on Saturday mornings so I carried on playing football with nobody on the touchline, just other people's excited parents chatting to each other. Dad must always be busy at weekends. If it was a big game he'd come, he said. He must have decided they were all small.

I swung and twirled on the swing until I'd finished my fish and chips and then made my way back up the road.

A message from Mum: How are you, love? Are you eating properly? Can we Skype? Are you getting on OK with Patti? How's the baby? Noisy, I bet.

I'm OK, Mum. Yes, I've got lots to eat. Patti is worried cos the baby has colic. What's that?

Colic is like a sore tummy babies get.

Did I get colic?

No, I don't think you did. But it is very common. Miss you!! But I'm making the most of the sunshine.

It's cold here. I deleted that. Instead I wrote, Are you having a rest? Guess what, I got made a prefect! I take people on tours of the school. I get a badge and everything.

New message: So proud of you!

Back at school, I hung around behind the trees by the gates and watched Mr Dunlop and Miss Reynolds walk across the car park to go home. Soon Mr Rafferty appeared in the infant playground at the front of the school, sweeping up leaves and covering over the sand trays. Five thirty. Quick Cricket Club must be finishing. There were loads of kids in that club. I sped down the path to the school office among all the parents and bikes and skateboarders and sneaked in as all the kids from the club were surging out.

If someone saw me, I was all ready to say, "Oh yeah, I was in Cricket Club and I've come back for my homework." I marched inside, turned the opposite way to the crowd and ran down the corridor. No one saw me. I spotted three people in red shirts from the cleaning company and heard hoovering coming from the library. In my head, I went over Mr Rafferty's words. The cleaners would still be around until six thirty; that's when he did his rounds and checked each room. Dunlop had already gone home, so my guess was I could hide in our classroom, but when I popped my head round the door there were murmuring voices inside. I went to the art room instead. The lights flickered on. I crawled behind the recycling bin and looked around. This room had already been cleaned. All the art materials had been put back on the shelves and it smelled of chemical lemons. My phone said five forty. I put it on silent.

The lights went off.

I sat for a whole hour, listening out for voices. It got chilly and I rubbed my arms. My legs hurt. I stretched them out very slowly. The lights stayed off. I held the bin in front of me like a tummy. There were flaking bits of paint around the sides.

If someone peeped in I would look like a bin with legs. The hoovers hummed. It got dark outside. The school fell silent. A door clunked shut. I heard voices in the distance.

A noise outside the door.

The art room door swished open. As the lights flickered on, I pulled my legs back in and crouched behind the bin, as tense as a cat. My heart throbbed inside my chest. Don't move. Don't breathe! Near the door came the sound of a table being shunted.

The door closed. Footsteps echoed. I breathed a long breath out.

The lights clicked off.

I carefully stretched my arms and legs again.

Success! I'd have my own adventure holiday. Just like Mum.

I could climb out of our classroom window and hang off the apparatus. I would sleep in the library. There weren't any automatic lights in there so I could move around as much as I wanted. But first I'd wander round the little cabins in the trees and pretend I had a garden. I would like a garden. Dad's house with Patti has a garden. His new family can play in it.

Chapter 10
Callie

We all sprang in the air, then we were off and running back across the playground, feet pounding, hearts thudding like crazy. Past the apparatus. Into the trees.

I scrabbled desperately. "The hole's gone!"

"It's here, you banana," came Nico's voice.

His arm shot out and grabbed me, and I squirmed under.

Safe on the other side, in my garden, the three of us panted and laughed. "Who do you think that was?" Zara said in a still-panicky voice.

"The lights come on in some classrooms automatically, don't they?" Nico said.

"But someone has to trigger them. This was at the end near the hall. Must be the library," I said. "What would start moving around in a library?"

"A teacher?" Nico said.

"It's nearly half past seven. They've all gone home. And anyway it was dark inside school before that," Zara said.

"Maybe they were saving electricity," Nico said.

We all burst into giggles again. My heart was still thundering. I felt like we'd had a lucky escape. But from what?

"Are there any lights on now?"

Nico stood on tiptoes, craning over the fence. "I don't think so. Could have been a cat."

"Switching a light on?"

"No, tripping a sensor thing, you nitwit!"

"Or Mr Rafferty?"

"The caretaker? He doesn't live in school, does he? He would have gone home by now. Anyway, why would he suddenly check the library? It doesn't make sense. He wouldn't just check one room. It must have been some kind of security light."

"Serves us right. We shouldn't have gone," Zara said.

"It was fun, though," Nico said.

We ran back up the garden and pushed open the kitchen door.

Mum, Ollie and Chloe were inside on the sofa cuddled round a book. The air smelled of washed hair. "Aren't you cold, you lot, staying down in that summerhouse? Did you put the heater on?" Mum called without looking up.

"Yes," I said.

"No, we didn't bother," Nico said, both at the same time.

We stood still for a second.

But then Mum just laughed. "Help yourselves to a drink if you want one."

Chapter 11
Ted

I knew it was time to climb down. It was cold in the tree. Everything was dark. Nothing else was going to happen. I'd been watching for ages.

I thought of the animals up here – squirrels, birds. I liked animals. I had spotted a badger under the bushes near the fence in a shaft of moonlight a few days ago. It was amazing. Badgers are secret night visitors too.

Although I was the quietest of quiet, the badger knew I was there, but it went on digging. Badgers are violent. The earth was flying. I watched its long nose and stripes. "Are you looking for a worm?" Next morning the tree roots would be all scratched and raw. It was magnificent. Silently, I edged nearer, listening to the tiny grunts and snuffles. I stayed as still as a bug and waited until the creature disappeared under the fence into Callie's garden. He waddled, he actually did; his bum was wide and his legs were little. He swayed from side to side like a boat on legs. Some people say they were an animal in a past life; in that case, I would choose to have been a badger.

I decided to feed him. I buried a sausage in the garden, not too deep, so the badger could come back and collect it later.

I shivered. I had watched the others run back up the garden. They had all been so excited about going into the playground. Even though it was just a playground.

Except... At least you didn't get pushed off things at night – you had them to yourselves.

They never looked up in the tree; I could have been doing gymnastics and they wouldn't even have noticed.

Callie was laughing so much when they all ran up the garden.

I'd wanted to tell Callie about the badger and watching it dig. I could have shown her where I'd first seen it. Now I'd never get the chance.

I climbed down and wandered back up the garden to bed.

Chapter 12

Callie

I lay and thought about tonight and the hole under our fence, then I got out of bed and went to the window. My school lay silent on the other side of my garden fence. That was really fun, going inside the playground in the dark.

School didn't feel the same now; it felt like … a place for mysteries.

Chapter 13
Billy

I liked the library.

I lay on the beanbags staring up at the walls. The beanbags smelled pongy from all the kids who had flopped on them in library lessons. Beyond the dark playground were the fences and behind those the dark shapes of houses. I'd been using the torch on my phone but only a little bit.

At night, the whole library turned green. My arms and legs turned green too, like being under the sea. The infants had made monster mosaics for the walls, from plaster and broken cups and plates. Some had eyeballs on legs. They gleamed and glinted. The eyes seemed to move.

I didn't mind being among the books. I'd found the one on rockets I'd chosen in library period, but it felt wrong to take it off the shelf. I could put the librarian's desk lamp on again, but that was too bright. It felt risky.

I shuffled right back into the corner where the extra-spelling people get taken and tested every week. I never get any better at spelling, but I like being taken out because Miss Austen's nice and she waits for us to try longer than Mr Dunlop does, sounding out the words.

There was a whirring electrical sound, as soft as

a whisper, coming from the corner by the corridor. Buruppppppppppp, buruppppppppppp.

I know the home noises. When I go to bed, Mum is always up for ages and I hear her moving about – the sigh of the kettle coming on, cupboard doors squeaking and closing. Often, Mum is on her phone. I like hearing her laugh; my mum's got a great laugh. It's a kind of low chuckle. She often rings Stella and her voice drops as she chats. They have known each other since they were at school. Stella's like family, Mum says.

Sometimes Stella comes over and they laugh so much until Mum goes, Shush, don't wake Billy. But I don't mind.

Normally Mum finds a lot of things funny but she isn't laughing very much these days and there are dark circles under her eyes. The other night I heard her say to Stella, "If I don't get a break soon..."

I made my eyes shut. The whirring electrical noise must be the photocopier sleeping. People use it all day; no wonder it gets worn out.

I was a bit worn out.

So why couldn't I sleep?

I wouldn't look at the monsters on the walls. A

school was just bigger than a flat, that's all, with more furniture and rooms and electrical things.

A message came: Hot and sunny.

Mum must be really happy.

And then another message: Where are you sleeping at Dad's? Are you in Kingsley's room? Is that working out OK?

I stared around me. I'm trying different places, I wrote. There's more space than I thought.

I added a smiley. I'm getting used to it. Love you!

Chapter 14
Callie

Next morning, I was ready for school early.

"What's going on, sausage?" Dad called, walking around with his bowl of cereal. "You're never up!"

Dad's usually the first awake in our house. He works as an electrician and he often has an early call-out before the rest of us are dressed and downstairs.

He grabbed me in a hug and ruffled my curly hair until I pulled away.

"I just felt like ... having lots of time," I said.

"Well done," Dad said. "Hey, Mum told me about the prefect thing. Maybe if you're always early..."

"It's OK, Dad," I said. "I'm not that desperate to be a prefect."

When Dad had gone, I nipped down to the end of the garden and laid some garden refuse bags across the hole under the fence, dragging them from the shed and plonking a big flower pot on either side. If anyone came down here now, they would think we'd been planning a den. I don't know why I bothered really; Mum and Dad were far too busy to come here anyway. I suppose I really wanted the hole under the fence to still be there when I got home tonight.

On the way to school, Zara caught up with me on the main road.

I linked arms with her. "Let's tell Ted about yesterday," I said. I liked telling Ted about the things we got up to.

"Of course," she said.

We caught up with him by the bus stop.

"Something exciting happened yesterday," I told him.

His face brightened.

We told him about the hole under the fence and going inside the playground. He nodded.

"What time did you go in? How long for? What did you do?" Ted always remembers things really well.

He nods as if he's writing it down inside his head.

"Out of my way!" came a sudden cry behind us.

We leapt to the sides of the pavement. Families with buggies and little kids sprang apart. It was Nico, flying past on his skateboard. There was a bang just inside the gates followed by angry voices.

"Nico's in for it now," Zara said. "Dunlop's on gate duty!"

We followed the massed hordes inside the playground. Nico was lying in a heap with adults looking down at him.

The bell went.

Mr Dunlop came striding over with a very red face. "Inside!" he shouted at Nico. "This minute!" He marched Nico through the school doors and the rest of us lined up and followed.

In our classroom, Dunlop made a massive scene about the extreme danger posed by skateboards and the selfishness of some pupils who think they can just do what they like in the playground and crash into the sensible people dropping off their children.

"I am astonished. How many times do I have to warn you, Elm Class, about being thoughtless with property?" He beckoned Nico and grabbed the skateboard. "You will not be seeing this again for a long while, young man."

He pointed to a list on the whiteboard that said 10 minutes' silent reading / lunch boxes / coats and he disappeared with the skateboard.

Whispers and jokes began. Mr Dunlop always

wants us to be grown-up about coming in without talking at all. I stuffed my lunch box on the trolley by the door, hung up my coat and got my reading book out, then went to sit at my table. Next minute Dunlop was back, without the skateboard, slamming the classroom door. Nico sat with his head in his hands.

Billy Feldon dived into the seat beside me. His hair was even wilder than usual. "Hey, what did I miss?"

"Shush. You have to be on time, now you're a prefect," I murmured.

Billy grinned. "Oops. I forgot!"

I watched Ted on the other side of the class, putting his things away. He saw me and did a little smile. I wished he could have come in the playground with us yesterday evening.

All day in school, Nico whined on and on about his skateboard. He didn't actually knock anyone over, he said, and anyway, the parent he crashed into had laughed. He said Mr Dunlop shouldn't be allowed to confiscate a skateboard – that it was against his human rights. Nico is always talking about his human rights. He's obsessed with them. "How long's he going to keep it for? It's mean.

Bet I don't get it back for weeks."

"You could ask your parents to complain to Mrs Alexander?" I said to him at playtime. She's our head teacher. "Maybe then you'd get the skateboard back faster."

"No, because my mum and dad would agree with Dunlop," Nico moaned. "Mum says I never take enough care when I'm on it. I'm doomed!"

"I wonder where he's put it," I said.

"Probably burned it in a fire. Or smashed it up. Or sold it. He could do a car-boot sale with all the property he confiscates!"

Nico did have a point. We'd all noticed the way Mr Dunlop reacted and confiscated stuff as a punishment but then forgot and kept the things for weeks. I think that was because there were so many people to punish in our class, he just couldn't remember all the threats and confiscations.

Nico went to ask for his skateboard back at the end of the day and we all stood listening.

Dunlop said, "I want to see a real change in you, Nico, before I even think about returning that skateboard, so there is no point in asking. Do I make myself clear?"

You can't say No you don't when a teacher says Do I make myself clear? It's not a real question.

As the four of us wandered out of the school gates at the end of the day, Nico fumed, "Dunlop can't do this to me."

"He can," I said. "I think you'll just have to wait."

"Well, thanks!" Nico said. "Big help you are."

He stomped ahead up the road.

We waved goodbye to Ted and he disappeared down the path to his house.

Nico was waiting by my front door and he jogged back up the path. "Hey, Callie, I just thought, my skateboard is bound to be in the PE cupboard. That's where Dunlop would put it."

"So?"

"So we could sneak into school again tonight and get it back."

I stopped walking. "Well … couldn't you just go back and check now?"

Nico threw his hands in the air. "I can't go now! There's clubs in there. And cleaners. I could never look for it during the day either; the hall has indoor PE and assemblies. And it's where the infants have their lunch. Someone would be bound to catch me."

"Mmm," I said.

Chapter 15
Callie

Nico wouldn't give up.

We swung on the tyre and played in the garden until tea. He gazed longingly across the fence as the sky grew darker. "I bet my skateboard's in that hall cupboard. Why don't we go in and get it later when your mum's gone out?"

Mum always does a supermarket shop on Wednesdays and takes the younger ones, leaving us in the summerhouse or watching TV. Our neighbour Mrs Dukes is happy to call round if we have any problems, which we never do.

Nico's face was alive with hope. "Five minutes, Callie; we can go straight to the hall."

"How do we know the hole under the fence is still there?" Zara asked.

Nico hopped around. "I've just checked. Come on, Callie. It'll be easy. We'll climb in your window."

"It's not my window." I sighed. "Someone might catch us inside."

"The whole building is empty," Nico said. "Anyway, if there was someone, we could run out again really fast." He grinned. "It would be fun to go in again!"

That was never going to persuade me!

He turned grumpy next. "If you won't come, I'll have to go on my own. I can't live without my skateboard." His face turned, full of misery. "You don't understand..."

I couldn't bear it. "I do understand!"

"So you'll come? Look, ten minutes, then I'll never ask for anything else in my whole entire life."

Zara was shaking her head. She bit her lip. "Well, I'm not going. It's wrong," she said.

"Taking my skateboard was wrong," Nico said.

"You crashed into loads of people," Zara pointed out.

"There weren't that many. And I said sorry," Nico said.

Zara looked almost tearful. "Well, I don't want to. Going inside is different. It's ... breaking in."

Nico hit the tyre and it swung violently. "We won't break anything. And the window's loose."

"The window might have got fixed," I said.

I felt stuck. I did feel sorry for Nico, though. He looked so tortured.

"You're supposed to be my friend," he said.

"I haven't said no," I said softly.

He grabbed my arm. "Yay! You'll come?"

I nodded. "All right. But we have to be quick."

"Bags of time!" he said.

We all watched Mum like hawks. Ollie and Chloe were being a pair of pains; they fought with a spoon for the mashed potato and ended up thwacking it across the room and spattering the toaster. Mum was furious. Then she bundled them into the car for the supermarket shop, calling, "I'll be at least half an hour, love."

"No rush!" I called back.

We watched as the car pulled away.

Ten seconds later we were sprinting down the garden.

We didn't say much. The hole behind the summerhouse was still covered by the sacks and pots. We tore them off and jumped inside.

"I'll watch for the car coming back," Zara said. She hovered anxiously. "And I'll keep checking the time. But be quick."

We popped up on the other side of the fence and sped through the playground, making for the classroom window.

"Result!" Nico said. He paused on the windowsill. "Hey, Callie, what if an alarm goes off?"

"Put your leg inside and waggle it about," I suggested.

He yanked it fully open, straddled the windowsill and waved his leg. Nothing. He did a thumbs-up and jumped down inside.

The lights came on. We nipped across the room and out of the door. The lights snapped off behind us. I flicked on the torch on my phone. It wasn't completely dark; there were glass panels along the roof. We stood with the junior classrooms on both sides and glinting model balloons wafting around over our heads. Just us and the silence. The emptiness felt weird, like something terrible must have happened to all the people. We couldn't speak in normal voices and kept stifling giggles. We set off down the corridor, past the ICT room and down to the school hall.

The hall felt vast. The floor gleamed. It smelled of vegetables from all the lunches that got served in there. Nico ran to the PE cupboard and pulled open the door. His voice was muffled as he rooted about. "My skateboard must be in here. Dunlop can't have taken it home."

Bangs and clatters came from inside the cupboard.

"Hurry up," I called.

But I was starting to enjoy myself. The wall bars beckoned, so I hung off one. I didn't climb high. It felt worse being inside school than when we had run round the playground. I felt like a robber. Or a spy.

Nico came out of the cupboard muttering, "Skateboard's not here! I can't believe it. I was so sure."

I leapt off. "We'd better go," I said. "It was worth a try."

"Wait." Nico's eyes gleamed. "What about the staffroom?"

"Nico! We can't."

Nico ran across the hall to the furthest doors, calling, "I'm going. I'm taking back what's mine."

Chapter 16
Callie

The light from Nico's torch was gone as the doors swished shut.

"Wait for me," I hissed, leaping after him.

The staffroom is right at the other end of school. I zoomed along, past the office. Seconds later I found him by the door marked Staff only.

"Dare you."

"You first."

"No, you!"

We pushed the door.

"Oh, wow!"

The first part was a kitchen. My phone torch lit up a bowl of fruit on the table, then across the room – fridges, microwaves and cupboards. I looked inside a cupboard and saw lots of brightly coloured mugs. Further in, pigeonholes for post lined one wall behind the long central table.

"It's really posh in here," Nico whispered. He stared at a line of lockers. "My skateboard wouldn't fit in one of those."

He started lifting up cushions then feeling behind the coats hanging up.

Along both walls were chairs, in lines, like in a doctor's waiting room. Nico rummaged underneath. "Move your legs, everyone," he called. And then, in Dunlop's voice, "That Callie is a waste of space. Elm Class are just the worst."

I couldn't resist doing it too. I perched on a chair. "Well, I'm disappointed, Elm Class. No team points for any of you."

Nico was still feeling around. "There's all sorts of stuff under here." He pulled out a pair of high-heeled shoes and then... "Look!" In his hand was one end of his skateboard with its lime-green logo. He waved it, beaming. "Under a chair. Like some junk; not even cared for. Dunlop's just slung it under here."

"What about when he looks for it?" I asked.

Nico jumped to his feet. "That's his problem."

I swung the torch beam around.

At the other end of the staffroom, something sat on the worktop by the sink. I went to check. It was a cake, a chocolate one with some kind of fudgy topping. Several slices had already gone. I found myself standing beside it. Chocolate cake's my favourite. A beautiful chocolate cake, not even put away, sitting out with a knife lying beside it.

"Whoever got it out didn't even put the lid on."

I chopped a bit off and crammed it in my mouth. My mouth filled with rich chocolatey sweetness.

Nico took a handful of a collapsed bit. We stood there stuffing our faces. If there's a chocolate cake at home, there's so many of us it's gone in a few seconds. This one was... Well, it was very good.

But then an awful thought struck me, enough to make me gag and stop eating. "Hey, Nico, cakes go dry. If we have cake at home, we always put it straight back in the tin."

"So?" Nico licked his lips and reached for some more.

I had a really bad feeling now. "Everything else has been put away and wiped and cleaned. Mum and Dad would never leave a cake out. And what about mice?"

"I don't care. It's good cake," Nico said.

"But don't you see? That means someone was eating this cake, like ... recently."

"So?"

My mouth was dry. "I think someone's still in school, Nico. That's what the cake means. No one would just leave this out unless they were going to come back for some more."

We both looked at the staffroom door.

"But if a teacher was still here, why didn't they turn the proper lights on?" Nico's voice wobbled.

We looked at each other. A person in school who wanted all the lights off. My insides turned to jelly. "Someone weird is in school, Nico," I heard myself whisper. "The cake's a sign!"

Chapter 17
Callie

We belted down the corridor, Nico clutching his skateboard to his chest, our torches making the wall displays leap and dance. Down past the library … round the corner.

"Argh!" We hit something. Something human-sized.

As I stumbled and fell, the figure squealed and Nico's skateboard hit the wall – kadung!

My phone skittered away.

There was a terrible shocked silence.

I scrabbled for my phone. Nico was quicker.

The beam came up. A teacher?

No … my height.

A face.

Billy. Billy Feldon. He was staggering to his feet.

"Billy!"

"Callie!"

"You."

Nico's torch lit up Billy's gleaming eyes in the gloom. The three of us gaped at each other, like creatures frozen in car headlights.

"Hi, Callie." Billy held on to the wall. "What are you doing here?" His hands shook. He swung them forwards and backwards. He wasn't wearing a coat.

The pounding in my chest slowed. "Why are you in here?" I said.

"I asked first," Billy said. He seemed to think for a moment. "Thought I'd be early at school for a change," he said. "Joking!"

Nico laughed.

Billy hopped around. "It's creepy, isn't it? Hilarious. Dunlop might jump out. I reckon he lives here, regenerates every morning in the office." He was talking very fast. He looked strange; gazing around and behind us, his hair wild. I looked down. He didn't have any shoes on either!

I pointed. "Where have your shoes gone?"

"I, um, took them off." He grinned again. "S'nice and cool ... with no shoes."

"How did you get in?" I asked.

Billy hesitated. "Same way as you."

"No, you didn't," Nico said. "You weren't in Callie's garden. You couldn't have come under the fence."

"Oh, no, no, course not." Billy's eyes narrowed. "Ha ha. I've got a special way in."

"We came to ... collect something," I said. Nico whipped the skateboard behind him. But

Billy didn't look like he was listening.

"So why did you come in?" I asked.

"Um... A bet. Yeah. Someone bet me I couldn't get inside school and wander around for a while."

"Who?"

"Um ... Sami."

Sami was a boy with a groaning sort of laugh who Billy hung around with.

"So where is he then? Is he here too?"

"Erm, no. Somewhere ... outside." Billy's eyes flicked left and right. "Maybe he ... left."

"So how will you prove to him you got in?"

"I'll text him. I'll take a selfie."

"It's dark. That won't prove anything."

His eyes jumped round. "Did you go in the staffroom? Did you find the cake?"

"Yeah."

"There's loads of food in the fridge too."

He was still hopping about.

"What were you doing in the library?" I asked.

His eyes flicked again. He grinned. "Oh yeah. I was taking back a book."

My phone pinged. A text. Zara. "Get back here!"

"Is that Zara? We should go," Nico murmured.

Billy stood his ground. "I'll just wait till you've gone, then I'll..."

"You never said how you got in."

"Come on, Callie. We've gotta go!" Nico said. "We promised."

Billy blocked my path. "Don't tell anyone you saw me. I mean, otherwise I'd have to say I saw you!"

He slid away. Back towards the library.

Nico and I legged it down the corridor, across our classroom and out of the window. Seconds later we were running across the playground to the fence.

Nico passed the skateboard over the top to Zara. "You were ages!" she said. "It's twenty-five past."

"Can't believe my skateboard's home," Nico said.

"You can't ever take it into school now, you know," Zara said, like a parent.

"I know that. I'm not stupid! I'll leave it in the summerhouse. Just for a few days. I'll use it at home or on the skateboard park. No one will ever take it away from me again."

I paused for a second. "And, Nico, we can't tell

ANYONE we went in to get it. Nobody. Agreed?"

He grinned. "Yep."

"Of course," Zara echoed.

Nico went off to hide the skateboard in the summerhouse and came back to join us. We sprinted up the garden and pushed open the back door. Seconds later, Mum's car was reversing into the drive.

We all burst out of the front door to help bring the shopping bags in.

Mum said, "What a lovely lot you are. Thank you."

We each grabbed a bag and Mum unclicked the car seats for my brother and sister.

"I hope you haven't been playing outside all this time. You must be perished. It's getting wintry," Mum said. "Let's get this shopping unpacked. Then we can all have a slice of chocolate cake."

I caught Nico's eye. He grinned.

"If I eat any more chocolate cake, I think I might be sick," I whispered.

A few minutes later, in the kitchen, Mum cut us huge fat slices. I gave my bit to Zara. "Not you as well," she hissed. "I just ate Nico's bit!"

Mum saw. She took one of the slices back and

her face filled with concern. "Callie, what's wrong, love? This isn't like you at all. Are you feeling OK?"

I kept picturing Billy's terrified face in the torchlight. And that threat – Don't tell anyone or I'll have to say I saw you!

"I'm fine, Mum," I said. "I just don't fancy any cake. I don't know why."

"I'm loving it, Mrs Evans," Zara said.

I thought about Billy again. My head was full of questions.

Inside for a bet. Taking back a book? No shoes?

You didn't fool me, Billy Feldon, I thought. You're a total liar.

Chapter 18
Billy

I looked in my overnight bag to find the football hoodie Dad got for me and hugged it. My special United one. It felt so soft, almost like fur inside. I shouldn't have brought it from home, but it kept me warm. That's why I slept in it last night too.

That was fun meeting Callie and Nico. They'd never tell on me. But the school seemed emptier once they'd both left – the long corridors, the little noises. I'd watched them climb out of our classroom window and run across the playground and disappear into the trees.

Message from Mum: How's the food, love?

It's great. I can have all the cereals in one bowl. And chocolate cake!

When I was curled up on my beanbags in the hoodie and the fleeces from Lost Property, I started to think of her and my eyes kept snapping open. Bumping into Callie and Nico in the corridor must have jangled me. I saw her face in the monsters on the walls. My weekend at Dad's just wouldn't go away. I switched on the librarian's desk lamp and pushed the head right down so there was just a glow, and tried closing my eyes again.

On Sunday evening, I'd been at Dad's. I'd spent all day with the screaming baby, and Saturday night had been OK because I'd had the room to myself. But on Sunday, at teatime, K came back. Dad was on the phone to the doctor for advice and the baby was thrashing around and twisting and screaming. No one really spoke to me.

Patti spent the whole time trying to soothe the baby. "You two, sort out some food for yourselves, will you?" she said.

I grilled some fish fingers, but when I got back from the loo, I looked for them and found them in the kitchen bin. In the end I ate a bowl of cereal.

K sat down opposite me at the table and flicked open a can of drink. She put headphones in and hummed.

It was hard to swallow. She glared at me – a raw, violent stare. I think if she could have cooked me, she would have done it.

In between slurps of drink, her thumbs pounded her phone. I couldn't help staring at her dark, smudgy eyes. Those chains round her neck must be heavy. Her chin was sharp. Her mouth drooped.

Her head jerked up. "What are you staring at?"

I got away as soon as I could. But where could I

go? Dad was on the phone in the lounge with the baby and Patti, and he'd told me to make myself scarce.

I stood in the hall at the bottom of the stairs, then I pushed open K's bedroom door. The space was tight but I had managed OK with the bunk beds last night. The walls were dark and she had closed the curtains. There was a smell – a dark, perfumey smell, like candles and spices. I had put my overnight bag here this morning, up on the top bunk, but when I looked, it was gone.

I wondered if I'd left it in the kitchen. I went to look. When I came back, K was in the room. Her lip twitched into a sneer. "You can't stay here." Her voice was flat. "Ooh, look, your bag has left already." Her eyes flicked to the open window and the pulled-back curtain.

I guessed she'd thrown my bag out. Coming out of the front door, I found the bag and all my stuff scattered across the front garden. My hoodie was spread over a bush. One of my shoes was in a plant. I bundled up as much as I could find and went back into the house. In the bathroom, I changed into my pyjamas and cleaned my teeth.

Back in K's room, she had moved to sit at her

desk with her back to me, and the top bunk was now covered in her books and clothes.

I stayed in the doorway. "Where can I go?" My voice came out small.

She turned. "NOT ... MY ... PROBLEM." She spat each word separately. She was completely still, like she'd been frozen into a statue. Except for her eyes. Her eyes boiled.

She really hated me! I was like a zebra, accidentally in the lion's cage.

"Bedtime, you two," Dad's voice called.

Maybe if I was very slow?

I gently started moving all the books and things off the top bunk, piling them on the floor, watching her. So far so good. I climbed up on to the bunk. I tried turning to the wall, but I didn't like not seeing her, so I turned back – I had to know what she was doing.

Suddenly she crossed the room and her strong fist yanked my head back, her nails scraping my scalp. "Why are you still in my room? Huh?"

I spluttered and choked. "I don't know." My hair felt on fire.

She let go. Bonk. My head hit the pillow.

"You will not touch anything. You will not move

anything," she said.

She turned back to her desk and fiercely hammered on her laptop.

I lay still, too scared to move.

A long time passed.

The light went off. My bunk shook as she got into bed below me.

"You'll never sleep," she said.

Then a noise began that sounded like an animal chewing.

I think she was grinding her teeth. The sound made me want to climb out of the window and run home. I was stranded; I couldn't get out to go to the loo and that made me want to go a lot.

Somewhere nearby, the baby went on wailing, like a bird.

I felt like wailing too.

I tried to picture Mum on the aeroplane, but it was too difficult, and she was moving away from me ... further and further. I told myself next Saturday she would be home again, but then I found myself thinking about Dad because it always used to be me and Dad at football on Saturday mornings. Everything and everyone was gone. I was ambushed by sad things. I was gulping. I couldn't help it.

"Does the little baby want his mummy?" said Kingsley's mocking voice from below me.

Light blazed in my eyes. She'd switched a lamp on.

I looked up at the ceiling and tensed. I could hear muffled sounds and movements below me.

"It's raining, it's pouring!" Cold drops hit my face.

I leaned over and found myself staring right into mad green eyes. Kingsley lay with her finger gently tugging the trigger of a water pistol shaped like a rocket. I leapt back. An arc of water shot up.

"Is the little baby crying himself to sleep?" She swivelled herself to sitting and perched on the edge of her bunk. Another jet of spray shot up, soaking my pyjamas.

"Leave me alone!" I said, shielding my face as another shower hit me.

"Oooh, please ... please ... please!" she whined, mocking me.

She was up and standing over me, moving the water pistol closer, directing the jet right at the middle of my forehead. "Target practice!"

A pain like drilling between my eyes. My heart

hammering. Bright water fountaining off my face, filling my mouth and eyes.

"I told you you'd never sleep!"

I was soaked and shivering. "Please stop! Please!"

✗

Tonight, in the dark library, I felt as if I could still hear that wailing baby and the teeth grinding, right by my head. I shivered tight inside the United fleece, remembering the water spraying sharp and cold between my eyes.

You will never sleep!

I froze myself, as still as still. I mustn't make a sound. Maybe, somehow, she could come and find me … even here!

Chapter 19
Callie

I couldn't sleep. Meeting Billy like that in the corridor – I kept picturing the look on his face. What was he really up to?

I couldn't get him de-prefected, he was right about that – not without explaining why I was in school as well.

When Zara and Nico had gone home, I borrowed Mum's binoculars and went down to the bottom of the garden in my fleece and wellies. It was a clear chilly night with lots of stars. I trained the binoculars on the school and slowly swept them across.

Through the trees, the playground lay like a grey slab with the blocks of the school behind. The whole place was in darkness, except for the glowing lights on top of the scaffolding, near the gates.

Then I saw it – a faint gleam of light in the library.

What if Billy hadn't come out when we were leaving? What if he was still inside our school?

Nico just assumed that Billy had come in for a few minutes, same as us. But I knew Billy. The way he had behaved in the corridor, asking us lots of questions to stop us asking him. I always suspected Billy of making things up: messing about, saying he gave something to a teacher when he didn't, signing slips himself for activities, telling me, "My mum's too busy."

My sister Chloe slept in the bed beside mine, snoring softly. I could hear Mum's and Dad's voices downstairs. I always went to sleep to the sound of their voices. Should I go downstairs and say, I'm worried that someone in my class is sleeping in school?

I climbed off the bed and stood there in the dark. I must be wrong. Billy wouldn't do that. He was just a joker who made me laugh. The glow must be a security light that came on when a cat walked by. But didn't those turn off again after a while?

And why hadn't I noticed it before?

I hadn't looked with binoculars before.

I thought of Dad saying, "What is going on in that head of yours? Get to sleep and stop making up things to worry about."

I've always been a worrier. When I was little, one night I screamed out and told Mum and Dad that the ceiling was going to fall on me. When they put the light on, we found a really thin wobbly crack running all the way across and Dad said,

"Cracks in the ceiling are normal in old houses." He shunted my bed a little bit more into the corner. "Now," he said. "That's you sorted. Nothing is going to happen and even if it did you're not underneath the crack any more." Then I went to sleep. Next day, Mum and Dad painted over the crack in the ceiling and it had never come back.

After all these years, my ceiling had never fallen down. Dad's voice seemed to ring in my ears. "Stop making up things to worry about."

I lay down again and pulled the covers tight over me.

I felt my eyes closing.

Chapter 20

Ted

Today was a bad day in school.

Mr Dunlop had picked me out. "Stand up. Right then. Necessary. Spell it out for me." He leaned back in his chair and rubbed his hand around the back of his ear. "Why is it necessary for all of us to wait for you to open your mouth and answer the simplest question?"

Some people laughed.

"Don't worry, we've got all day."

The class waited.

My skin prickled. Heat rose inside me.

People were looking at each other. Sighing. Poking.

Over by the window, next to Callie, Billy Feldon was telling a joke. It must be about me trying to spell. Callie laughed. I wished I could be like the badger and dig an escape far away.

"N ... E ... S..." I said at last, trying to imagine the word in the air.

"Can't hear you," Dunlop snapped.

"N ... E ... S..."

"No! Again."

"N ... E ... C ... S..."

"Nope. Again."

"N ... E ... C ... E ... C..."

"Give me strength! Again!" Dunlop thumped the desk. "Just be brave for once."

Tears had come then. I tried to picture the word, but it wouldn't stay still in my head.

Hands went up around the room.

"Put him out of his misery, someone!" Dunlop said.

Necessary...The word had spun around in my head all day. There was a rhyme thing, to do with sandwiches, maybe. Callie had tried to teach me it. Never eat cakes – that was it. What was the rest? Why couldn't I remember the rest?

Callie and Billy sitting there laughing together about me.

Safe in my tree, I looked down through the leaves into the next-door garden with the empty summerhouse.

Usually I climbed back down – foot ... hand ... foot ... gripping ... gripping ... feel around ... slide. But tonight I shunted along the branch instead and jumped down into Callie's garden; this garden where I was banned from going. My heart beat fast inside my chest. I had so much energy, I could leap on to the tyre and swing and swing but I didn't. Instead I jumped down inside the hole by the fence.

Why shouldn't I explore the playground too?

I flew around for a while and noticed a glow at the far end of the building by the library. I prowled closer. My skin prickled. A figure, curled up. Someone was asleep in the school library.

It was Billy!

Billy was the reason everything went bad. Billy the prefect. Billy who had laughed at me and made Callie laugh too. And here he was, sleeping in the school library!

This was a chance…

"I will be back!" I told the night air bravely.

Chapter 21
Callie

Next day, walking to school, we didn't see Ted to walk with. Maybe he was a bit late. Nico caught up with us, though.

"So are we agreed, we don't tell anyone about going into school last night?" I murmured to Nico and Zara.

Nico had a huge smile on his face. "Relax," he said.

"I think we should show the caretaker and your parents the hole under your fence, Callie, so they can fill it in," Zara said.

"Oh," I said. "Maybe not quite yet."

I needed to understand if something was going on first. I needed information. I deliberately changed the subject.

"So glad you like chocolate cake, Zara."

She grinned. "Not that much!"

Before the bell went, I jogged over to the field and found Sami in goal. Sami's all right. He'll normally help you, if you ask him. If you said, Hold the end of this bench, he's the kind of person who would just say, Yeah, OK. He's very strong and he's a good runner. And he always laughs at jokes in our class, with a kind of groaning frog croak that annoys our teacher a lot.

"Hiya, Callie," he said.

"Are you goalie?"

Sami was leaning against the goalpost. "Sort of."

"So Billy won your bet then?" I said.

"What?" His eyes widened.

"Your bet." I watched him closely. "Last night?"

"I don't know what you mean." He jogged away to the other side of the goal.

I followed him. I don't think Sami wanted to talk to me. He was going to, though. "Were you and Billy together yesterday evening after school?" I asked.

"Who says we were?" Sami plunged his hands deep in his pockets and jogged up and down. "I've got to watch the goal, Callie."

This wasn't true. All the action was up at the other end and, anyway, everyone knew the bell was about to go. Someone had got a second ball out and started juggling it.

"I'm just asking if you were with Billy. Yesterday?"

"Might have been," Sami said.

I waited while he squirmed.

I knew he'd crack. "No. I was at my nan's," he said at last.

"So you didn't see Billy?"

"He doesn't live near my nan."

"You didn't dare him to do something?"

Sami shook his head. "No. I went to the cinema."

The bell went. Sami looked relieved.

We jogged back to the playground to join our class. "What film did you see?" I called.

"The one with the goats. The zombie one."

"Was it good?"

"Yeah."

Sami slowed down just as we got near the line. He turned nervously back to me. "Billy broke the food mixer, Callie," he said in a low voice. "Otherwise, he could have stayed."

"What mixer?"

"At my nan's," he said. "See ya!" And he jogged away to the back as everyone fell silent.

My brain churned. Otherwise, he could have stayed. What had Sami meant by that? He hadn't said it as a joke; he'd looked uncomfortable. I knew Sami would help Billy if he could.

I was close to something. I could feel it. It must be how detectives feel when they find a crack in the witness's story.

I watched Billy. He had always been "slippery" in school, crashing into people and calling, "Lost my balance!" He loved a mess too, and he was always there grinning when paint was getting spilt. Today in class he seemed even more like chaos on legs. His uniform had more creases in it than usual and his hair stood up at the back as well as on top.

While we were supposed to be drawing a map of a trench, my mind kept wandering. Maybe Billy was a thief. Maybe he was part of a criminal gang, smuggling out computers? Dad told me a whole lot of equipment had disappeared last year in the summer holidays. Had Billy been about to steal something when we had met him in the corridor? Imagine if I unmasked him and saved my school thousands of pounds. They'd definitely make me a prefect then.

But I still had this feeling he had spent the night in school. How did that fit? Thieves didn't usually stay in the place they were robbing.

I found Billy at break. He was on the wall, watching the football game. "Why were you really in school last night?" I asked him.

"I was having a party," he said, winking.

"That's rubbish and you know it. Why don't you answer?"

His face went serious and for a second I thought he was going to say something real. Then he said, "Banana for a nose or oranges for ears?"

"Billy!" I said.

"When they squeezed your ears, they'd get orange juice," he said.

"Not talking to you," I said.

He nodded. "Fine. You can't tell anyone about me, though. You'd get in trouble too. We'd all be for the chop!" He put his teasing face on again. "Hey, did you eat some of that chocolate cake in the staffroom?"

I nodded. "Yes. Was it you who left the lid off?"

"I was planning second helpings."

"Oh."

That really didn't sound like a burglar.

"Do you think our teachers have cake every day?" Billy licked his lips and bit into a huge slice of imaginary cake.

"Billy … what's going on?"

"No wonder they rush to the staffroom and say they have a meeting."

He just wouldn't stop joking. But when he

wasn't looking, I noticed he kept yawning, and his head kept sinking down on to his arms in class.

Ted was sitting outside by the planter in our usual place. I was glad to see him. I can always talk to Ted. We often sit together while other people are rushing about, chatting about everything that's been going on in our class.

"Hiya," I said, perching beside him.

Ted turned his eyes on me. His face was serious today. "Callie, yesterday in the evening, did you go back into school?" he asked.

Something did a jump inside me. "No," I said, thinking quickly.

Ted frowned. He was looking at me strangely. "But if Nico's got his skateboard back...?"

My heart jolted. "Oh ... yes ... well ... um...!"

"So if Dunlop didn't give the skateboard back, how did Nico get it?" He waited.

I felt my face flush. "I don't know... I... Um... I think maybe Nico did go in and get it."

"But not you?"

"No."

Ted's face turned sort of ... wounded. He got up and walked away.

I thumped the side of the planter and got a

splinter in my thumb. Ow!

I'd lied to Ted for the first time ever.

When he'd gone, I realised one of the reasons I'd lied was because we'd met Billy in the corridor. The other reason was that we said we wouldn't tell anyone. I'd kept quiet about what had really happened. But there was something about the look Ted had given me. I got up and paced around the back of the goalposts.

Ted really hated Billy. I was right not to tell him. But I felt so tangled up. Ted is one of my best friends.

When I mentioned it to Nico, he said, "That was stupid, telling Ted that you didn't go inside school yesterday."

I grabbed his arm. "Hang on, Nico, we agreed we'd keep last night a secret."

"You're weird, Callie," Nico said. "Anyway, it's too late. I've already told Ted we both went in and got my skateboard back."

"What?!" Now I was blazing mad. "But we agreed. We said we wouldn't tell anyone!"

"Ted's our friend. He's not going to tell anybody; he wouldn't do that."

"But I just told him I didn't go."

"Then you are a prize prawn."

"Did you tell him we met Billy?"

"No, course not."

The whole thing was so stupid: Normally I could trust Ted more than Nico. Ted was a quiet kind of person; the sort of person you would trust to keep a secret. I wasn't sure about Nico, though. One time he told Zara that I'd eaten the chocolates we got for her birthday because he thought it was funny, which it was, but Zara was really hurt. And I was really cross. And it just turned into a horrible mess until Mum made us all sit down and say sorry. And it was my fault for eating the chocolates. I bought her some more in the end. Now Nico had got me in real trouble with Ted. I could feel it. I was going to have to say sorry and explain.

Chapter 22

Callie

I found Ted again sitting on the wall, looking out across the field.

"Ted, look, I didn't tell you about Nico's skateboard," I said, "because I just wanted to keep things secret."

"You could have still told me the truth," Ted said softly, shaking his head.

"I'm sorry. I thought we'd agreed not to tell anyone – like, not anyone at all."

Ted looked down at his feet. His lips hardly seemed to move. "So that's how you think of me," he said. "Just anyone."

"No!"

"You lied to me." He got up and walked off again.

I'd been thinking for ages about how to help Ted and cheer him up. Now I'd really upset him instead.

The day got worse. Nico just couldn't stop celebrating having his skateboard back. He kept whispering stuff about Dunlop in class.

Our teacher was in a foul mood all day. Before lunch, Dunlop caught Richie texting on his phone, went silently up to him and barked, "Why have you got your phone when you know phones are to be handed in to the school office at the start of the day? I'll take that."

"He'll probably just throw it somewhere in the staffroom," Nico said loudly, from the back.

I froze. I looked across at Zara and her mouth was wide open.

Dunlop swung round. "Was that your voice I heard, Nico Kendal?"

My heart was in my mouth. My breath stopped.

"No, sir," Nico said.

"You're sure you didn't add your dulcet tones to the conversation I'm having with Richie?"

Nico shrugged.

Later on, in afternoon registration, Nico actually went up to Mr Dunlop and said, "Mr Dunlop, when am I going to get my skateboard back?"

What was Nico doing?

"You'll get the skateboard back when you have shown me that you can be wonderfully silent and hard-working," Mr Dunlop said.

But Nico stood his ground. "I thought we got confiscated things back at the end of the day, but this is the second day."

"I am aware," said Mr Dunlop, his lip curling in a sneer.

You know that voice teachers have that says *Don't push me any further.* Dunlop was doing that voice. But it seemed like Nico just didn't care.

Later, when Mr Dunlop was talking to another teacher by the door, I grabbed Nico as he walked past my table.

"Why do you keep nagging Dunlop about your skateboard?" I hissed.

Nico's jaw set. "He shouldn't have taken it."

I threw my hands up. Unbelievable! "But we got it back!" I mouthed.

Nico shrugged. "Dunlop doesn't know that."

I grabbed his arm. "Nico, if he starts looking for the skateboard in the staffroom, he won't find it, will he?"

He shook me off. "Duh! Exactly. Serve him right. He'll have to buy me a new one."

My mouth fell open. "But then you would have two," I hissed.

Nico's eyes glinted. "That's OK. I'd like two," he said.

"Nico, you have to stop winding Dunlop up."

"No, I don't. Whose side are you on?"

"But we got your skateboard back, that's the point."

Nico's mouth spread into a grin. "Make him sweat. He'll think he lost it. It'll be epic. This is the best fun I've had in ages."

When we went to the library to change our reading books, Billy sat on a beanbag and had a huge illustrated book about outer space across his knees.

I like library periods. I like browsing through the books and gathering a whole pile before I choose which one to borrow. Next time I looked over at Billy, his eyes were closed. He was fast asleep.

I shook him.

He started up and did a huge yawn.

Mr Dunlop must have noticed because he came over. "I didn't bring you here for a snooze," he said.

Billy was as quick as a flash. "Ooh," he said. "I thought you did. This beanbag's so comfy."

"I don't want to hear from you," Dunlop said.

"I'll go back to sleep again then, shall I?" Billy murmured, as Dunlop walked away.

A load of people laughed at that. I laughed too because sometimes Billy is so fast-thinking. It's like he says it for everyone.

And I think Mr Dunlop should have checked

that Billy was all right – like, talk to him on his own or something? I mean, he is supposed to care about us.

There seemed to be so many things to worry about. Dad sometimes talks about fighting fires in a day; you sort one thing out and then another worry jumps up and hits you. In afternoon play, when I found Zara, she had worry lines right across her forehead.

"You and Nico should never have gone into school to get that skateboard back, Callie," she said.

Not this again!

Her voice was firm, like she'd decided something. "Nico just wants to get Mr Dunlop into trouble." Her lips pursed. She turned her deep, serious eyes on me. "I feel like the hole under your fence was a test, Callie, to see if we would be tempted to do a bad thing. We should tell a teacher everything."

"We can't!" I almost shouted.

"We should," Zara said. "Even if we get in trouble for it."

I was amazed. Zara was about to make things even worse! I had been going to tell her my worries about Billy but now I hesitated. Zara could drop us all in it.

"Let's just wait a bit?" I said carefully. "I'm sure it will all calm down."

"I'll think about it," she said.

Don't, I thought.

Everything felt tangled up and terrible: Nico almost bragging, hinting about what we did, Zara wanting to confess to a teacher at any moment and Ted thinking I wasn't a proper friend and didn't trust him. All afternoon, I felt the chill of him staring at me across our classroom.

And somewhere at the back of it all I really hated the idea of us getting into massive trouble for going under the fence and into school. I suppose I still did really like the idea of being a prefect. And I didn't want Mum and Dad and the teachers to think I would do a thing like breaking into school.

But I did break into school, didn't I?

When we walked home, we all ignored each other. Ted disappeared without his usual wave. Back at my house, I told Nico not to play on his skateboard in front of the other kids or let my mum and dad see it.

"Well, if that's how you feel," he snapped.

"Yes, it is how I feel," I snapped back.

Nico sulked in the summerhouse. He treated the skateboard like a pet, smoothing the curved sides, running the wheels across his palms. It should have been hilarious, but it wasn't. Zara practised maths questions. "It's the Maths Challenge tomorrow. None of you even care," she said. She got out a Maths Made Easy book and worked on it like a person doing an exam. Zara can be the most boring person in the world sometimes!

She was right; I didn't care about the Maths Challenge. She was annoying me. Not as much as Nico, but definitely annoying.

Just before tea, Zara looked up from her book and said, "Let's tell your mum about going in school. Let's just do it. Get it out of the way."

Nico looked at her as if she'd suggested flying to the moon. "Why would you tell an adult, Zara? That's idiotic!"

"Because what we did was wrong."

Nico pretty much boiled over. "They'd make me give my skateboard back. Dunlop would keep it for the rest of the year! Anyway, you're just as much to blame for going under the fence the first time."

"You persuaded us."

"You've got a brain, Zara! You chose to go in the playground."

"Not the second time. Not when you and Callie went inside."

"Ooh, Goody-Goody Miss Perfect. Whose side are you on?" Nico roared.

They snapped and sniped at each other. I just wished they'd go home.

We didn't tell Mum. We arrived in the kitchen to chaos – Chloe had bashed her knee skidding on a plastic truck that someone had left in the hall. We ended up clearing all the plastic toys into a crate, laying the table and helping put out food.

"You're all quiet," Mum said brightly, when Chloe's screaming had died down a bit. "Thank goodness for my sensible big ones."

We're not sensible, I wanted to shout. We're not sensible at all!

Chapter 23
Ted

Billy had started this thing with noises. It used to be a hum but then Billy changed it.

"Psss," he said under his breath, looking straight in front, lips pulled back. "Psss."

It was pretend peeing. It was aimed at me.

I turned redder and redder.

"Who is making that noise?" asked Dunlop.

We looked around to the left and right.

"Don't know, sir."

"No idea, Mr Dunlop."

Someone else started it next. "Psss."

*

A bad person should be punished.

I prepared for a mission.

First the big torch from beside the back door.

"What are you doing, love?" Mum asked, looking up from her laptop.

"Collecting things for a project."

"Oh, OK. Bedtime soon."

I found the ball of garden twine that Mum used for tying the roses. I thought of spiders making webs. When I wrapped it round my fingers, it left red lines.

It was late evening, long after bedtime, when I went to the school again. Climbing up, up, up, and along, and dropping down the hole in Callie's garden, squirrelling under, and running across the playground.

At the classroom window, I climbed inside. The classroom was still and quiet. I took off my shoes and left them by the window. My heart beat hard. The light clicked off. I thought of people sleeping in beds, and the badger padding around, searching for food.

To the library. There was Billy, under the librarian's desk, warm and sleeping inside a red hoodie.

Gently, gently, I pushed the library shelf on wheels nearer the sleeping figure. Trundle … trundle. Then I wheeled the other shelf the same way to make walls.

Boxed in.

Twine time. I spooled out a long length and wrapped it round a chair leg, then across the shelf, then over by the door and round the handle. Back … forward … around … across … up. A web!

Time to leave.

Back down the corridor … cool floor under my feet … across the classroom … rolling out of the window with my shoes clutched to me, pulling them on. Now outside, to the wide library window.

I wanted to write a message on the window but it would have had to be mirror writing, and I'd tried practising but it was actually really hard, so I did it on some cardboard instead, with fake blood running down it, and leaned it against the window.

I'm coming to get you.

Ketchup works OK, but it was hard to write with and I got a lot on me. I used it as drips instead. I'm coming worked all right but the other bit got squashed up and the letters filled up with ketchup, so it looked like, I'm coming to pet you or even I'm coming to sel you.

Fear scrunched inside me, like a fist. Get on with it, I told myself.

Interrogators use bright lights to scare prisoners. I pushed my giant torch up against the library window and flicked it on – crunch. It lit up my sleeping enemy like a car headlight. He sprang awake. His eyes were wide.

Got you!

Billy was like a rabbit when they freeze in fear as he saw the terrifying message. He didn't stare at it very long, though. It took ages to make; he should have looked at it longer.

Not laughing now. Not grinning and teasing and laughing now.

Billy went crazy, fighting inside the web of twine, all tangled up and stuck behind the bookcases, leaping, staggering and falling. Ha! His hands ripped at the tangled twine. He was all desperate and stumbling, until he'd got it all off him and forced the shelves apart.

I ran round to see what happened next. Only just in time to see Billy run across the playground and disappear into the trees.

I followed, glorious in victory.

Under the trees … creeping round all those little cabins where kids play at lunchtime. Where had Billy gone?

Wait… Where?

Under the fence?

I shook with anger. Something clicked in my head. How had Billy found out about the hole under Callie's fence?

Chapter 24
Callie

That night, I had a dream. The hole under our fence turned into a chasm, like the crater of a volcano, and me and my friends all fell down inside it, arms and legs waving and flapping. Quicksand oozed around our legs. None of us could move or pull ourselves up the sides. Terrified, I flapped helplessly, trying to wade over to Zara where she clung to the edge, but my legs were swept away, and as I spun round all the familiar friends' faces turned into Billy Feldon. I couldn't help anyone. I was gulping, drowning in quicksand as it filled my mouth and nose. Bleugh!

Tap tap.

I coughed and blinked. Suddenly I was properly awake. Tap tap. Something was hitting my bedroom window in real life. I jumped out of bed and looked outside. A person in a bright red hoodie, trailing school uniform sweatshirts, was dancing up and down in our back garden, right underneath my window.

Billy.

He saw me and waved.

What on earth?

Billy! How? Why? What was Billy Feldon doing in our garden?

I checked my sister Chloe, asleep with her teddy in her arms. She never wakes up. Dad says you could play a whole brass band next to her head. But in the room next door to me was my brother Ollie. He has asthma and sometimes wakes in the night for his medicine. I pulled on my sweatshirt and leggings with extreme care, then opened my door and crept out and down the stairs.

I turned the key in the back door and tugged it open. A blast of cold air hit me, and Billy was standing there on the step. His hair was wild. He was sort of half wearing several school sweatshirts and he didn't have any shoes on. His wild staring eyes searched my face like a trapped animal. He stepped towards me. "Please!"

Cross words died on my lips. He was crying. Billy isn't a boy who cries – he's a boy who laughs.

"Don't tell anyone," he sobbed.

"Wait," I whispered. I put my finger to my lips. "Shush!"

Mum and Dad sleep in the attic room. They wouldn't hear us – I'd tested my noise theory before when I was hiding Christmas presents. But one of my brothers might still wake up.

I let Billy in. He sat in the kitchen chair and shook.

Something big was happening. Something that needed some thinking.

Hot chocolate – that would help. Mum sometimes makes us mugs of hot chocolate if we have a bad day.

I closed the kitchen door then warmed some milk in a pan and splashed it into two mugs with chocolate powder in. Billy watched me like a hunted animal. I collected a pair of my wellies for him from the hall, took the key for the summerhouse and beckoned him to follow me.

We sneaked down the garden. I held the mugs gripped in one hand and unlocked the summerhouse door with the other. Billy sat on the sofa and squashed himself smaller against the beanbag, wrapping fleeces round himself. I thought he would speak, but he didn't. The summerhouse felt chilly and damp, so I switched the heater on.

It was strange. I wasn't actually surprised to be sitting in the night drinking hot chocolate with Billy Feldon. Some part of me must have guessed he would come and find me.

But the crying… He was still crying. I didn't know what to do about that!

Chapter 25
Ted

I sat in my trusty tree, waiting for Callie to throw Billy out.

Time slowed down. Nothing seemed to be happening; it was cold and sad and boring.

Was Callie calling her mum and dad? There was a light on in the kitchen. Would anyone come back down the garden?

I ducked behind the leaves as two figures came across the grass towards me and went inside the summerhouse, closing the door behind them. I could see them both inside but I couldn't see their faces, not without climbing down.

Inside my chest, anger broke in a tidal wave. Callie had been carrying mugs. She hadn't called her mum and dad or anything. She and Billy were having a picnic!

Callie wasn't going to do anything. Billy wasn't even getting in trouble.

Why? I moaned to the empty air.

Callie had lied. She had told me that she hadn't gone into school and I knew she had.

She was not loyal. A traitor of the lowest kind, in fact.

Why hadn't she thrown Billy out?

Chapter 26
Callie

"We can't put the light on – someone might see it from the house," I said.

Billy looked so odd; it was as if he'd walked out of my nightmare and into our garden. "We have to make sure the door's closed properly. Once a fox got in here and chewed the rug and pulled the cushions all over the floor."

Billy just stared back at me, bundled up in sweatshirts.

The silence was scary. I talked more. "We all sit in here after school. We do homework. I've never been in here in the middle of the night, except once when we camped in the garden and Dad was in a tent with my brother and sister so that doesn't really count."

Still Billy sat. My wellies, sticking out on his feet, were pale blue with sea creatures on. Billy could have been a stranded creature washed up on a beach. In school he was always moving, twitching, messing about with things. I didn't know he could stay still like this. I felt as if something dark was in the summerhouse too, making the hair prickle down the back of my neck.

"Drink the hot chocolate while it's hot," I said.

Billy reached out for the mug and sipped a bit.

"You mustn't tell anyone," he said.

"I won't."

"Swear."

"I'm not sure I—"

"Swear!"

"OK, OK, I swear. Where did you get all those sweatshirts?"

"Lost Property."

"S'like an octopus costume," I said.

He didn't even smile. Tears ran down his cheeks. You don't think of a boy like Billy crying. Some people cry easily, like my sister Chloe. Sometimes she cries just to get more pudding.

"Am I safe here?" he whispered.

I nodded. What a weird question. We both gazed around us. I didn't feel very safe now that Billy had said that. It was only our garden, but it felt as if someone might be watching. I shivered too. The heater takes a while to make the summerhouse feel cosy. It would feel better soon, I told myself.

We sipped. Billy wiped his mouth on one of his sleeves, still not looking at me. His eyes gazed out into the dark night sky outside instead.

"I can't go back," he whispered.

"Back? Where?" I asked.

Silence.

I decided to tell him what I already knew. Then he could add in the extra bits. I didn't look at him, just at the baggy cushion beside him. "Billy, I know you didn't really go inside school for a bet, because I checked with Sami and I think you've been staying in school at night. You're in the library, I worked that out. So, you see, you don't have to tell me. I know."

His eyes fixed on mine. "She's found me," he said. "I only just escaped." Now he talked quite fast. "I can't be at my dad's. That's where Mum thinks I am. But I went and ... I can't stay there."

He cried harder.

"Billy," I said. "Explain properly."

Billy knows me. It couldn't be that scary to talk to me! He sniffed and choked and started to explain in a voice that was hoarse and soft. "Um ... my dad moved out in the summer. He didn't tell us Patti was going to have a baby. It was Dad's. A little girl."

"So you don't live there with your dad's new family?"

"Of course not." His mouth twisted. "I live with

Mum. She's a nurse. Except now she's away on holiday. I'm supposed to be staying at Dad's until she's back."

"So when me and Nico met you, why were you in school?"

"Dad had to go away for work. And there's not just Patti and the baby; there's Kingsley. She's Patti's older daughter." He shuddered.

Kingsley's an unusual name. But the weird thing was, I'd heard it before. Someone had said it ... recently.

"How old is Kingsley?" I asked.

"Thirteen."

Thirteen... I remembered suddenly where I'd heard it. "She's not Kingsley Poulton, is she?"

Billy squirmed. "Yeah."

"Your new big sister is Kingsley Poulton!"

He looked horrified now. "She's not my sister. She'll never be my sister."

It all came back to me. My brother Elliot had said that name. In our kitchen. Not in a good way. I looked at Billy all hunched and shaking. "Kingsley Poulton's a legend at Larks Cross. My brother says, Kingsley Poulton did this in a lesson or Kingsley Poulton did that to someone's bag, like on and on. Everyone's scared of her. She's in his class."

Billy sighed. His head hung down. "Yeah, well, she hates me. There's only her room to stay in. It's completely terrible."

"So that's why you've been staying at school?"

"I was, but now she's found me."

He shuddered. His shoulders started to shake. "What am I going to do?"

"When is your mum back?"

"Saturday."

"Oh. That's not long."

"It's two more nights," he said.

"Isn't there anywhere else you could go?"

Billy rolled his eyes. "If there was, I wouldn't be here, would I?"

"OK, OK, don't get angry with me."

"I wasn't."

We were quiet again. "Could I stay in here tonight?" Billy said.

I sat up.

It was just like in school when he borrowed my things. But he wasn't like the Billy in school. He wasn't laughing and he wasn't joking. He looked … smaller.

"You said it was safe in here."

"I know, but..."

"So can I stay?"

I sighed. "OK."

Chapter 27
Callie

When I was back in bed, I thought properly and got worried. Had Billy been telling me the truth? Those things he said about Kingsley scaring him in the library and writing messages on the window?

Was Billy's mum really on holiday? What if he was making everything up?

But I had seen the marks on his hands from tearing at the twine.

Should I bang on Mum and Dad's bedroom door and tell them the whole thing?

But I'd sworn to Billy that I wouldn't tell anyone. And I could just guess what Mum and Dad would do: ring the school, contact Billy's dad, get all of us in massive trouble, get Nico's skateboard re-confiscated FOREVER! Make Billy's mum not have the rest of her holiday. My head filled with the voices of people shouting. And another quiet voice in my head said I'd never be a prefect if the teachers found out about all the things I'd done, and the night visits into school. Everyone would think badly of me; all their good opinions would get reversed.

And Billy sleeping in our summerhouse... Well, no one needed to know, did they?

Now I would be keeping secrets from everybody.

Even though Billy wasn't my friend, he was sad and he did need my help. The way he'd cried – that was real. I realised I'd never known him at all. Not really.

✗

When I came downstairs on Thursday morning, Mum was on the warpath.

"What did your last servant die of?" she called. This was one of Dad's expressions. "There's a pan in the sink and a spoon. Have you been having hot chocolate, Callie?"

"Oh yeah, I, um, made some," I said.

Mum was staring at me hard. "In the night?"

"Yeah. I just ... couldn't sleep."

"Is that all?"

Did Mum know there was more? I sort of froze. Mum just stood there, waiting. When she does that it always makes me start talking. "It's just, I've got some ... worries, you know."

Wrong thing to say. Mum put the tea towel down and her hand came down gently on my sleeve. "If you have worries, Cal, it's better to share them." She was looking at me in that earnest way she has.

Now what was I going to say?

"I'm a bit worried about … Ted," I said. "He just … won't talk to me." I prattled on. "I think he's … not very happy."

Mum frowned. "Ted's always been on the quiet side."

"Our teacher is always having a go at him."

"Oh."

"He's really not talking to anyone."

"That's a shame. You two have always been such good friends." She smiled. I knew she was remembering the mother and toddler group she used to take us to. Mum loves remembering us when we were little. She just likes small children. I guess that's why she enjoys being a childminder.

I felt bad now. I wanted the conversation to stop. I didn't like lying to Mum. I'd ended up talking about Ted to stop myself talking about Billy. I was just trying to distract her.

My heart thumped.

"Maybe we should have Ted round after school some time," Mum was saying. "It's a shame we don't see him these days."

"Who?"

She frowned. "Ted."

"Oh, yeah."

"He's good with the little ones." She smoothed my hair. "And you and Nico and Zara." Her eyes twinkled. "You four are the maths boffins, aren't you? Isn't it the competition today? We had a message from the school about it."

I'd completely forgotten. "Oh, yeah, exciting," I said brightly.

"Great," Mum said. "I'm glad we had a chat, Callie. You must talk to me if there's something on your mind. And wash up the pan next time."

"Thanks, Mum," I said.

I felt bad, kind of squirmy. I was turning into a massive liar. Just like Billy!

Chapter 28

Callie

I ran down to the summerhouse and checked that Billy was gone, and folded his blanket. At least he'd remembered to turn the heater off.

There was no sign of Ted today when I walked to school with Zara. She said, "I've been thinking about what's happened about the hole and the skateboard and I'm really sure we should tell Miss Reynolds at break."

I pretended to think about this. "Look, Zara, it's the Maths Challenge today. Let's practise for it at break. But – " I pretended to have a sudden idea, throwing my hands in the air – "oh no – if they think we've been breaking school rules, maybe they won't let us take part."

Zara's mouth puckered. "Oh, Callie, do you think so?"

"Look, I'll talk to my mum and dad at the weekend about the hole under the fence. We'll block it in. It will all be over," I said.

Billy would be safe and back with his mum by then. I could just sort of happen to notice the hole this weekend.

Zara was smiling. "You actually will?"

"Yes."

"Oh, Callie, I feel so much better. It's been

really worrying me."

"Yeah. Me too."

"I'll leave it then." She linked arms with me. "I think we'll do really well. Most of the other teams don't know each other like we do."

Zara was all happy again.

When we all trooped into assembly there was a line of stony-faced teachers sitting behind the head.

Mrs Alexander stood up and looked at us all like a hawk. "When Mr Rafferty came into school this morning he discovered a mess in the library. Breakfast-club children, you are trusted to walk from the office without touching anything on the way."

I looked along the line at Billy. He had his eyes shut. He'd found his shoes, though. I wondered where my wellies were.

"Someone has also been wrapping twine around the tables and chairs. Acts of vandalism are rare in this school." Mrs Alexander had very piercing eyes. They swept the crowds. She would spot anyone looking guilty.

And Billy had been telling me the truth. Well, some of it had been the truth.

I sat very still. But you know how your face goes red even when you aren't guilty just cos you're feeling worried. I could feel myself going redder.

Her voice droned on. "Was someone in school early? If you know anything about this, please see your class teacher or come and tell me."

I looked at a patch of floor and rubbed at the varnish with my fingernail. A flake came off.

"Things have gone missing as well. If something is not yours, leave it where you found it," she said.

I looked down the row at Nico. Were they searching the school for his skateboard? He sat zipping and unzipping his fleece.

I had another thought: had something else gone missing in school? Had something else been stolen by Billy?

I must look like a beetroot by now.

We came trooping out of assembly and Zara murmured, "Did you go in to school again yesterday evening, Callie?"

"You know I didn't. You were at my house!"

She was studying my face. "You could have gone in after Nico and I went home."

"Why would I do that?"

"I don't know, but when they said about the mess your eyes went all fixed and your face was all squidged up."

"Was it?"

"You said it would be all over," she said. "But everything seems to be getting worse."

"That mess in the library was nothing to do with us. You can't blame us for that, Zara," I said.

When we got to class, Mr Dunlop did his horrible throat-clearing thing and said, "It's the Maths Challenge today. We seem to have the maths geniuses in this class. Don't mess it up."

How did Mr Dunlop manage to be horrible even when he was being nice?

A while ago I would have been so excited to be doing the competition, but today it just felt like an extra problem.

I found Billy at break and asked about the shoes. He said they were from Lost Property. "I hid the wellies. I'll give you them back later."

"Billy, you were telling me the truth, weren't you?"

He paused. "I couldn't be making it up." He held out his phone. "See?" On it was a photo of a woman on a sun lounger, with a beach behind her.

"Is that your mum?"

"Yeah."

"Where did you say she is?"

"Lanzarote. Believe me now?"

I nodded. I mean, she could have been anyone but he'd have to be pretty desperate to show me a picture of some other woman on a sun lounger.

I wandered around looking for Ted. I hadn't seen him to chat to and that felt wrong. I couldn't find him, though. I looked all around the field and in the school garden where we sometimes helped. Was he avoiding me?

Too late, I realised I'd promised to practise for the challenge with Zara. I looked for her now too, but the whistle went and I ended up back in class.

"Where were you?" Zara said when I found her. She sounded sour and annoyed.

"We don't need to practise. We'll be great," I said.

"You promised," Zara said. "Doesn't that mean anything?"

"I was trying to sort some things out," I said.

She flashed me a hurt look. "I don't believe you about anything any more, Callie. I might as well do the challenge on my own."

Chapter 29
Callie

As soon as lunch was over, competitors from other schools began arriving and Nico, Zara, Ted and me were told to sit round a table in the hall. There were twelve teams. Everyone sat chatting. Except us. I was glad to see Ted, but he completely ignored me.

A very excited man announced the names of all the schools taking part. Zara gripped the paper, ready to turn it over. Nico looked bored and gazed out of the window. Ted sat with his chair edged away from the rest of us. The man gave Ted a sheet just for him. "Here you are. You don't have to share."

"Choose a team name," the man called. "Think of a really fun one."

"What shall we pick?" I asked.

Zara said, "Anyone got any ideas?"

"It doesn't matter," Nico said.

"How about … The Cool Cats," I suggested.

"That's a stupid name," Nico said.

"You think of a better one then."

"The Night Burglars," Nico said.

"Shut up!" Zara said.

"Ready steady and … begin!"

When we turned over the question sheet, there

were hushed whispers all over the hall. There were loads of maths problems to solve and they had "odd one out" shapes and missing bits of jigsaws.

Zara began frantically writing. I could hardly see the paper. I leaned over her shoulder to look and tried to read the questions.

If I walk 300 miles with a pile of oranges and then I pick up blackberries from…

Ted jotted some things down but he didn't share them. He curled his fingers around his paper, shielding it.

"Can we share your answers?" I asked.

"They're just ideas," he said.

"But can we all see them then?" I asked.

"No." He glared at me. "Why would I help you?"

"Because we're a team!"

"Give it here." Nico grabbed at Ted's paper, tearing it.

One of the helpers came over and gave Nico a copy of the questions too. "You can pool all your answers at the end," she said. "Do try to work together though – that's the whole idea of the challenge, isn't it, guys?"

"I am not a guy," Nico murmured. He leaned over to look at Zara's scrawling. "Can't read it."

"At least I'm trying!" Zara's voice was shrill. "Just go away, Nico!"

"We all need to agree," I said. "We have to share the answers. What did you put for number three, Ted?"

"I left it blank."

Zara looked desperate. "I'm not working with you all. You are impossible."

"Why would it be two hundred and fifty?" Nico asked Zara, pointing to an answer. "That one's wrong."

"No, it isn't," she said. "I haven't got time to explain."

It just got worse and worse. We fought all the way through and in the end Ted worked completely on his own. I copied some answers from Nico's sheet on to Zara's but in the last few minutes she crossed some of them out. As we got ready to hand in our sheet, Ted rolled his answers in a ball and threw them away in the recycling bin at the corner of the hall.

He looked back at me with empty eyes.

He wanted us to lose.

The sheet we gave in was a total scrawl, and some questions had more than one answer written in the space. Zara was in despair.

*

They read out the final scores. We were near the bottom of the team board and the teacher said, "Never mind, guys. At least you tried your best."

"I did. The others didn't," Zara announced.

"Stop being perfect," Nico snapped. "It's only stupid maths."

"I'm not perfect," Zara said. "I just made an effort."

We couldn't be a team. We were more like enemies.

Chapter 30

Billy

"Well, Billy," Miss Reynolds said, stopping me by the office. "You are looking as if … your uniform needs a bit of a wash. How often do you have a bath or a shower at home?"

"Often. Like … so often."

I must have got dirty crawling under the fence. I rubbed at a mark on my sleeve.

"Great. Doesn't take long to have a bath. You'll feel fresher in some clean clothes. And it's better to look a bit more … spruced up, if you are showing people round the school."

"Mum's been … very busy," I said.

Mum hadn't told school about going on holiday. She said it was no one's business but ours.

"She's had a busy time, has she?"

"Just a bit. She's fine and everything."

"Shall I give Mum a ring?"

"I'm staying at my dad's till the weekend."

Miss Reynolds made a note in a little book. "Oh, I see." She paused. "And how's that going?"

"Um, my dad's got a new baby."

She made another note. "Well, that's exciting."

"The baby's got colic."

"Ooh, I remember when my daughter had colic."

"She screams."

"Keeps you awake?"

"Yep ... yep, she does."

I would ask Callie for a bath. I liked baths. I was good at being invisible in school. I could be invisible in Callie's house too.

I found some more clothes in Lost Property. There was a big table of uniform and other things outside the office. A mum was looking through them. "All these lunch boxes with no names! Unbelievable. Some people have money to burn." She turned to me. "What are you looking for, love?"

"I ... um, my sweatshirt."

"How about this one?" She held one up.

"It's ... not mine."

"It's got no name," she said. "It's yours now, isn't it?" She held out a pair of trousers. "Now, these ones are practically new! Well, go on then. There's no name on them."

They looked a bit big, but we found a belt to go with them, with a buckle shaped like a crocodile's mouth. By the time I walked away I had a whole new set of clothes. These new ones were miles better than my old ones.

Chapter 31
Callie

When I got home from school, we all went in different directions. Zara played with my sister and asked to see her books, and Chloe was thrilled. Nico sat in the summerhouse hugging his skateboard again. The other little ones rushed outside and played in the garden. I ended up mashing potatoes. I was glad to be away from everyone. They were all pains.

I had agreed Billy would come under the fence at seven thirty. When the others had gone home, I went down the garden and found him already lounging on the sofa in the summerhouse. He'd switched the heater on. "Someone could live here," he said.

"Not really."

"It's cool, though. Can I put the lights on?"

"No, it's too risky." No one would see that light from the house unless they walked down the garden, but it still seemed a bad idea. Like tempting fate.

Billy was really settling in. "Can I recharge my headphones?"

"Yeah." I pointed to the socket. "Over there."

"Can I have a bath?"

"Oh, I don't know... I suppose..." I thought of

all the people coming and going in my house. But today would be quiet compared to some evenings because my mum was out at a school meeting.

"I'll be really quick. You can time me if you want," Billy said.

"I'm thinking… Mum's out tonight. And my dad and my brother are planning on watching a thing on TV."

Billy grinned. "It'll be a piece of cake then."

"S'pose so. I'll message you."

"No rush." Billy stretched out on the sofa. He'd got loads of school sweatshirts in his bag, and the red and white hoodie on top. He lay back against a cushion. "Have you got any snacks?"

"I'll see."

It was weird; Billy was like my little brother or sister, asking for treats.

Mum went off to her PTA meeting, luckily, because she would definitely have noticed something odd was happening. But then Chloe suddenly announced that she wanted me to read her a story.

"I've got homework," I said, eyeing the clock.

"It's only for a little while, love," Dad said. "She

asked for you specially."

So I read her The Red Truck is Stuck three times and by the time she had shut her eyes it was nearly eight o'clock and Mum would be home at half past.

Ollie and Dad were downstairs chatting in the kitchen. I texted Billy and said Come round the front and I'll let you in.

About a minute later, he appeared. "Target in sight," he murmured.

"Up the stairs. It's on the right," I hissed.

Billy ran up the stairs. He sounded like a herd of elephants. I turned to follow him but Dad popped out of the kitchen. I swivelled round and rearranged my face.

"Who was that at the door?"

I held on to the banister and tried to look relaxed. "Oh, Dad, it was Zara. She forgot her coat."

Dad frowned. "Why didn't she call for it on the way to school tomorrow?"

"She just ... wanted it now."

"Oh. Well, it's your turn to unload the dishwasher, love. It says on the rota. Come on."

Help! Now Billy was upstairs in our house on

his own!

I dashed through to the kitchen and started grabbing things out of the dishwasher. Ollie was rooting around for crisps.

I worked fast, nearly dropping a cup.

"Careful!" Dad said, filling the kettle. A distant rumble started above our heads.

"What's that noise?" Dad asked.

All our eyes flicked up.

"Sounds like the bath," Dad said. "I don't get it; Chloe is asleep and the rest of us are here."

I stood there horrified. Think! "I started running the bath before you told me to unload the dishwasher," I said.

Dad gaped at me. "What... Why, Callie?"

"Erm... I wanted a really big bath."

Dad shook his head. "Callie, that's a terrible waste of water."

"Yep. Sorry, Dad."

He folded his arms. "Go straight up. Do the rest of this when you come down."

"Yep. OK."

"Now." Dad followed me to the bottom of the stairs and watched me run up so I had to go straight into the bathroom. Billy had thrown all the towels round him like robes and everything he had been wearing was on the floor. I caught a glimpse of a bare leg.

He opened the bathroom cupboard. "I like bubble bath. Have you got any of that?" he said.

I grabbed a bottle of something and thrust it in his hands. "You are the limit!"

Angrily, I switched the bath on again so Dad wouldn't wonder why it had gone off so fast and we mimed at each other. "You have to be quiet!" I hissed. "Just be quick!"

I pulled the door shut and crouched on the landing. No way was I staying in that bathroom! There were sloshing noises inside.

I waited. I listened out for Dad and Ollie, ready to dart back in again.

Five long minutes passed. Then the bathroom door swung open and Billy appeared. He looked hilarious; he had pulled on his clothes, with a rug from the summerhouse over the top, and a woolly hat and the blue sea-creature wellies.

"I smell like coconuts," he said.

I could hear Dad and Ollie laughing at the TV. I was still terrified of Dad coming out of the kitchen again. "Shut up! Go to the summerhouse. I'll come and see you later."

"Can we have hot chocolate again?" Billy whispered as we sneaked down the stairs and I pushed him outside.

"Just go."

"Whoa. It's cold out here!"

"Go!"

I sighed and leaned on the banister. Keeping secrets from my family was so stressful! And Billy acted like he owned the place.

Chapter 32
Callie

Somewhere at the back of my brain I knew there was something I had to do, but Dad must have heard me come downstairs and called, "This dishwasher won't unload itself!" So instead I rushed back into the kitchen.

Dad turned round on the sofa, looked at me, then looked harder. "Didn't you wash your hair?

I put my hand to my head. My hair was dry. Whoops! "Oh, I forgot," I said.

"Why didn't you put your pyjamas on?"

"I just," my voice wavered, "like my school uniform."

"So you put it back on?" Dad was staring at me strangely. "Callie, are you OK?"

"Yep!"

I started putting all the cups and plates away. A few minutes later the front door went and Mum called, "I'm back!"

Then my brother Elliot came slamming into the kitchen, home from a friend's house. "I just went upstairs to the loo. Looks like someone washed a dog in the bath," he said.

The bath! "It's me, sorry..." I said. I took off and sprinted upstairs. All the towels were on the floor and there were muddy footprints around the sides of the bath and a smear of scum round the edge.

Suddenly Mum was behind me. "Callie, what's been going on in here?"

We both stared at the scene of devastation.

My brain was whirring. "Erm… I washed my wellies in the shower over the bath. I used lots of towels because … it's an experiment about dirt and how you get rid of it." This sounded really pathetic but I tried to keep my face straight, as if it was a normal thing to say.

"Your teacher asked you to do this," Mum waved at the mess, "in your bathroom at home?"

I panicked. "No, no. I got the idea from a website."

"What?" Mum sank down on the bathroom stool.

I started scrubbing at the sides of the bath.

"Are you all right, love? I feel as if something is going on with you, Callie. This mess. Getting up in the night."

She reached for a towel from the floor, held it up, saw a big mark on it and dropped it back on the floor again.

A big sigh came out of me. Should I tell her about Billy? Tell her now. Then she wouldn't think

I was this weirdo who experimented with dirt in the bathroom.

"I... I..."

Mum waded across the towels and hugged me. "So, Callie, where have you put your wellies?"

"Oh ... I took them back, um, downstairs."

"Sarah!" Dad called.

Mum sighed. She looked meaningfully at me. "Something's going on with you."

I nodded, shook my head, nodded again.

"Oh." Her expression cleared. "I invited Ted for tea tomorrow, and a few neighbours are calling in. We'll have a bit of a bonfire party. Just a few of us."

"What. Tomorrow?"

"Yes, Ted's mum popped into the meeting tonight. It would be lovely to see him again. I thought you could toast marshmallows."

"That's so ... soon!"

Mum frowned. "Ted's mum suggested tomorrow. What difference does it make?"

"None," I said in a high squeak. "Thanks, Mum. Tomorrow's great."

I went back to cleaning the bath. Cleaning the bath was easier than thinking.

When everyone had gone to sleep, I sneaked down to the summerhouse with hot chocolate again, and the remains of Dad and Ollie's snacks. Billy was trying on his new school clothes from Lost Property. He held up a pair of school trousers and a belt with a heavy buckle, like a biting crocodile.

"Was that in Lost Property?"

"Yeah. They've got everything!" Billy said. "It's better than a shop!"

He pulled on the red and white hoodie he'd been wearing yesterday. The hoodie was an adult-sized one, so he could fit all of him inside it with his knees tucked up.

He seemed different after the bath. His hair stood up like a fluffy chick's.

"Do you always wear that hoodie?" I asked.

He stroked the sleeve. "It's unique, Callie. It's a United one. That's my team. My dad saw it in a raffle. We'd been to a match. It was an amazing thing because three of the players have signed it. Look." He sat up and pointed to the scrawled signatures on the front panel. "Dad got loads of raffle tickets and said, 'Come on, we're in with a chance, Billy. Someone's got to win it.' And when they announced our number, it was the best day of my life."

It just looked like a normal hoodie, but I was more interested now.

"They shook my hand and everything. Dad said, 'Well, it's yours. Probably worth a packet. Get your mum to frame it.' But we didn't. Mum forgot."

"Is it worth lots of money?"

Billy nodded and hugged himself as if he had a pet in there, like a rabbit or something. I don't own anything I care about so much like that, except maybe the earrings Mum and Dad got me last Christmas with the tiny blue stones. I've hardly worn them; they seem too special.

"If this hoodie was in a frame, I couldn't wear it," Billy was saying. "It's got a great hood. It's really warm."

We drank the hot chocolate and ate the snacks. I was glad we had the heater on; it was cold tonight.

"What's your baby half-sister like?" I asked.

Billy shrugged. "Small."

"How much hair's she got?"

"Just a normal amount. It stands up a lot."

"Like yours."

He put his hand to his head and flattened the hair down. His voice went sad. "Why didn't my dad tell us until after she was born?" His eyes were pleading.

"Maybe he didn't want you to be upset."

Billy made a little noise. "Hmm." His shoulders slumped.

"Maybe he forgot."

"You can't forget a baby, Callie," he said.

"Well, I don't know, maybe he was going to tell you and then he daren't. My mum didn't tell me she was having Chloe because I got so jealous when she had Ollie."

I remembered those days, when Mum never seemed to be at home. Ollie was born early, and Mum had to come home from hospital without him and go back to visit him all the time. She was never there to say goodnight to me.

Billy nodded. His eyes looked very big.

"When they brought Ollie home, I said I'm not having that in my room. Put him in the bin!"

Billy laughed. "Really? What did they do?"

"They cleared out the boxroom and put him in there. Babies are quite boring."

Billy slurped the hot chocolate. "Dad's one just

screams all the time. She's got colic."

"So do you pick her up and help with her?"

"I'm not doing that." He shuffled his legs around. "I haven't really been there. They don't want me there."

He looked as if he might cry again. I changed the subject and held out the crisps. "Billy, there's something that doesn't make sense. Yesterday, you said Kingsley came looking for you in school."

He nodded.

"Well, why would she do that?"

"How do I know? It has to be her. She must have followed me from their house."

"But why would she bother?"

Billy shuddered. "She likes making people scared."

"But she made you leave your dad's. She'd already won."

He sighed.

"Did you see her, when you got woken up in the library?"

Billy pulled the hoodie around him. "There was just a bright light in my eyes. I don't want to talk about her. It's hard to sleep if I think about her. I don't think she's human." He yawned.

I yawned too. I must go back to bed. I had to wash the pan from the hot chocolate, and the cups.

"OK, look, tomorrow evening my mum's invited some people. You might have to come a bit later. I'll let you know. You can still sleep here. It's just that you'll have to wait until they've all gone home. I'll text you."

He stretched out on the sofa. "I'll get fish and chips again."

He was in such a mixture of clothes: the hoodie, the sweatshirts, the rug, my wellies. He looked a bit helpless. I found myself saying, "It'll be all right once your dad's back, won't it?"

"He won't help. Dad's forgotten us."

"He's still your dad, though."

Billy shrugged.

His phone pinged. "'S my mum. Baseball cap or football?" he read out.

He tapped a message back. "Football. Love you, Mum." He checked his phone again. "She's asking if I'm OK." He tapped again and grinned at me. "She says she's bought both."

"What's your mum like?" I asked.

"She's sometimes fierce and sometimes silly.

I'm glad she's on holiday. She deserves it." He closed his eyes. "Night, Callie."

I stood up and there was Billy Feldon stretched out on our lumpy sofa. "I always thought you were really irritating," I said.

Billy opened one eye. "That's what Mum says."

"It's just … not everything's a joke." I thought about Billy spraying Ted with orange juice. "Like what you did to Ted."

"That was an accident."

"Was it?"

We looked at each other.

"I'm going to bed," I said. "See you tomorrow, Billy."

Chapter 33
Ted

I jumped down from my nest of leaves in the tree. Callie had gone back up the garden to the house. The laughing and chatting must be finished.

Could I smash the summerhouse windows? Or tear down the tyre and smash the goalposts? Something had to happen. Callie had chosen Billy as her nearly-brother.

Like a shadow, I moved right up to the windows and pressed my face to the glass. Billy was alone, and asleep. He had a blanket, but it had slipped. He wore the red hoodie over his clothes. The hood was up and his fist curled round the string. He was always in that hoodie.

No one should be allowed to make someone else look stupid. No one should steal another person's friend.

A brave new plan started to grow in my head.

Chapter 34
Callie

Next morning I checked Billy was gone from the summerhouse. The heater was off. The sofa cushions were squashed but I plumped them up.

Mum and Dad kept asking me how I was. They must have been discussing me. I left for school quickly.

As I walked up the road, Zara appeared beside me. She had been checking back through the Maths Challenge questions, she said. "That question about the fractions; I just don't understand why we were so slow at getting it." She wouldn't stop yapping on. "I bet the school never chooses us again."

I sped up until we were almost running. "Zara," I said. "Most people in our class wouldn't want to do that Maths Challenge if you paid them."

Nico appeared and ran alongside us. "Why are we running? What's going on?"

"Zara's upset. About losing the challenge," I said.

"I'm just saying..." She looked hurt.

"What are you just saying?" Nico asked.

"She's been going back over the questions," I said. Normally I listen to Zara when she talks about schoolwork, but today I had too many other things on my mind.

Nico rolled his eyes. "Zara, nobody cares about the stupid Maths Challenge. We lost. Why don't you give in all the correct answers to Miss Reynolds and tell her you're a maths genius and it was just the rest of us that were rubbish."

Zara looked like she was going to cry. But today I didn't have a go at Nico for being mean. I pretty much agreed with him.

We were almost at the gates now. "I'm taking my skateboard home tonight," Nico said. "I'll tell Mum and Dad that Dunlop gave it back."

"That would be an actual lie then," Zara said.

"You're not perfect yourself," Nico said.

"At least I didn't steal."

"How could I steal when the skateboard was mine in the first place?"

"It was still stealing."

"Stop it!" I said. "Just stop it, both of you. Stop bickering."

"It wasn't stealing. In fact –" Nico stood his ground and pointed sharply in the air like a teacher in a lesson – "I was reclaiming it."

That wasn't the sort of word Nico would ever use. We looked at him.

"What's wrong?" he said.

"Reclaiming?!" I started to laugh.

"Shut up! I was reclaiming it!" Nico looked back down the road. "Where's Ted anyway? He never walks with us now. He's gone weird."

And then we walked on into school in silence.

We all seemed to be "scratchy", like the littlest thing was making us snipe at each other.

In assembly they announced that the scaffolding would be coming down next week and the new windows fitted, and we all cheered. I'm not sure why we cheered, really, but if a teacher says something in an excited voice most people will cheer. I kept looking along the line to find Ted. I saw Billy. He looked smarter today; his hair looked better. He wasn't in his proper school shoes, but he was in shoes. And he was in a really good sweatshirt. His clothes actually looked better than they usually did.

I couldn't see Ted. The hall was packed. If you keep looking behind you, a teacher tells you off and points to the front. I hadn't properly talked to Ted in days. I realised I missed him. I missed our chats. Ted listened to what you told him and he seemed to really think about it.

Chapter 35
Ted

I had things to do. A quest. I found Billy's bag above the photocopier where I had seen him put it and hid it in a new and secret place in the music practice rooms. I was late to the hall for assembly, but it didn't matter; I could sit with Year Three at the back and no one would notice. My brave new plan moved in my head, ideas twisting and flowing. I smiled to myself.

Chapter 36

Callie

I scanned the class for Ted and got up to go and speak to him, but Mr Dunlop was in one of his Who is supposed to be speaking in this room? Is it you? No? Well, get out your reading book and zip it moods.

Ted never seemed to look in my direction all the way through maths and science.

At break, the minute I got outside Billy came to find me.

"My bag's disappeared. My big one with the blue stripe. I hid it before breakfast club. All my stuff's in it. Someone's moved it."

"How should I know where it is? I'm not your mum," I snapped. "Why didn't you hide it in the summerhouse?"

"I just wanted to keep it safe."

"And now you've lost it."

"It was in a good place, Callie. I put it in the costume store above the photocopiers."

I lost my patience. "You are such a full-time job, Billy! Look, I don't know where you put it and also why would I move it and also where would I put it. Maybe a teacher moved it."

He frowned. "Keep your hair on." Then he grinned. "Hey, save me some food tonight, yeah?

What's it going to be? So I can think about it."

Sometimes Billy Feldon seemed younger than my five-year-old sister! "It's usually sausages and burgers," I said.

Billy did a thumbs-up. "Great. Thanks, Callie."

It was Ted who I wanted to see. There he was, sitting on our usual planter, gazing into space.

"Ted!" I called, and went to sit beside him. "At last! I wondered where you were..."

My voice trailed off. He didn't make space for me. I was kind of wedged up against a green spiky plant. "Mum said she invited you to the bonfire evening in our garden tonight."

Ted sort of looked through me, as if I'd made a tiny sound he couldn't hear. He blinked. Then he stood up and walked away. As if I hadn't said anything at all. I watched him go ... round the edge of the playground ... up on to the field ... over to the village cabins and trees... I watched him until he was out of sight.

I had thought about so many ideas for helping Ted, but I'd lost him. Just because I hadn't told him about a skateboard? It didn't make sense. It must be more than that. Ted seemed hurt in some sort of big way. He seemed sad in the way people are sad about huge things happening to them, like when your cat dies. I realised Ted had seemed like that for weeks. He didn't seem like my friend any more.

Why? How did that happen?

I sat there with that plant jabbing into me, and I felt like crying. I never cry. There was no one to talk to for the first time ever. My friends had spun out like sparks in an explosion. Zara was hurt about the Maths Challenge. Nico was loud and irritating. Billy just wanted things. And Ted was like a stranger.

Chapter 37

Billy

I searched everywhere for my bag. I'd put it in one of the hatches above the photocopiers where they stored costumes for school plays. As soon as I'd got to school I'd put it in one of the hatches above the photocopiers, where they stored costumes for school plays. I've often put things there. No one was doing a play; it should have been fine. I didn't actually need any of my things until tonight, but I had to know my bag was safe. I should never have brought my hoodie. I asked Callie, of course, but she said she hadn't seen the bag. I checked Lost Property but there was no sign of it. I wondered if maybe Mr Rafferty had moved it, so I tapped on the door of his little office.

He appeared, looking suspiciously at me round the door. "Mr Rafferty, is anyone doing a play?" I asked.

"Nope, not until nearer Christmas. You should be in class, lad."

"I have to collect something, from the office. Um, is anyone moving things – like, having a clear-out?"

The caretaker frowned. "Well now, some things have gone walkies from the staffroom. People need to keep a better eye on their stuff and not dump it around the school. God knows what their houses must look like." He came out of the office and blew his nose so loudly that all the children doing spellings stopped and looked at him.

"Put your things in the boot of your car or in the cupboard in your classroom!"

I nodded. I think he'd forgotten I wasn't a teacher.

"Exactly," I said. "Erm, so have you seen a blue and white stripy bag?"

"Nope." He blew his nose again. "And I haven't seen a chocolate cake or a skateboard neither." He sounded quite annoyed.

"Thanks then, Mr Rafferty."

He grunted. It was a bit awkward because it was me who ate the cake and I'm pretty sure the skateboard was Nico. Dunlop confiscated that a few days ago so maybe a teacher moved my bag first thing this morning while they were looking for Nico's skateboard.

At lunchtime, I found Nico in the playground. We raced to the wall by the field and back a few times. I had to keep hitching up my trousers and tightening the crocodile buckle, so he won easily.

As we wandered back towards school, I said, "What happened to your skateboard?"

"I got it back," he said. There was a challenge in his voice.

"Dunlop gave it back?"

Nico chewed this idea for a second. "Not exactly." I could tell from his face that he wasn't going to say any more.

"Have you seen a blue and white striped bag?" I asked.

"Did Dunlop confiscate that as well?"

"Nah. Forget it."

I kept searching all through the day, whenever I got the chance. I even took a parent tour into the small hall to watch the aerobics so I could check under the tables where we have breakfast club. No luck. By the end of school I was getting a bit desperate. I kept thinking about Kingsley throwing my bag out of the window.

But then I found a message pushed inside my locker at the end of school.

Your bag will be by the new classrooms at 7.15.

I just knew it was Callie. She'd found it and kept it safe. Clever Callie!

Chapter 38
Ted

I held the red hoodie between my fingers, stroking the soft front panel where the names of the footballers were signed.

Then I bunched together old cardigans from Lost Property and packed the hoodie with them, mixing them with the shredded cardboard I'd found in the school recycling. Then I worked carefully on a face. It was made from a pale tea towel, pulled tight around an old cushion. The eyes were buttons from the button box, the nose was a peg, the mouth a dribble of ribbon.

I stood back and admired what I'd made so far. The figure had a puffed-out chest. It nodded when I pulled it upright. The legs were floppy, but I had tied the ends of the trousers with string.

Then I wrote a message and wedged it inside the locker. Your bag will be by the new classrooms at 7.15. That should do it.

Chapter 39
Callie

That evening I got home with Zara and Nico and we helped Mum make the bonfire in the back garden. Thank goodness we had something to do so we didn't have to talk to each other. The summerhouse was open and they switched on the fairy lights. We made buns and helped the little ones ice them. There were sausages and burgers cooking in the oven. People started arriving: neighbours; Benjy and Timmy's mum and dad; Elliot's friends from school. We gathered in the garden and the little ones ran around. Dad had come back specially early and was in one of those moods where he keeps spinning people round and running up and down the garden giving piggybacks.

Ted appeared with his mum. He carried a bundle and he was dressed all in black. He looked at me with narrowed eyes. I decided to leave him alone. Maybe he would talk to Zara.

Dad called me to help. We put music on and danced on the lawn with the little ones. But I couldn't help thinking about Billy and wondering where exactly he was right now. I knew he was going to find somewhere to hide in school until I said it was OK to come. But all the adults were chatting and drinking and I could see it was going to be a long evening – you know when adults start laughing really loudly and telling stories about family disasters and secrets we're not meant to hear; there was a lot of that.

I found Ted staring into the flames of the bonfire. I could just be friendly. Couldn't I? "Do you want a hot dog?" I asked.

"Why did you invite us?" he snapped.

"You're my friend. Anyway, my mum suggested it."

"So it was your mum. Yeah, right."

"Ted, what's wrong?"

He pointed inside the summerhouse. "This is where we used to all sit. You could sit in here … even at night." He stressed the words.

"Yeah … I suppose so."

We walked together right to the end of my garden and he pulled away the bags covering the hole under the fence. "A badger made that hole," he said.

"Did it?"

Something jolted in my head. The summerhouse at night…?

"I watched that badger. He's been in my garden

too. I feed him. He's like … a friend."

It was like Ted was with me but not with me. Like he was mostly talking to himself.

"Ted?"

He looked at me strangely. Then he plunged away into the crowd.

Nico was right – Ted had gone weird! I shuddered. His words reminded me of something, just out of reach. Something I must have known but not understood. What, though? A text arrived from Billy: Glad you found my bag. Save me a burger. See you later.

I stared at my phone. What did Billy mean? I hadn't found his bag.

Mum broke into my thoughts by asking me to get drinks for the little ones. The fire was blazing now. I'm always fascinated by bonfires. Lots of people were standing round it and each time an adult threw on more wood it snapped and hissed and sparks shot out. I stretched out my hands to warm them.

Zara appeared beside me. "We're going to toast marshmallows," she said.

In another bit of my brain there was a bright flicker of an idea. "Zara," I said. "Have you spoken to Ted? Is he in the kitchen?"

"He wouldn't talk to me," Zara said. "He just looked busy. And why's he dressed all in black?"

I suddenly wanted to tell her what had been happening and I blurted it out. "Zara, Billy is going to sleep in the summerhouse tonight. He's got nowhere else to go. He's in school now. He's coming later when the party is over."

Zara gripped my arm. "Oh, Callie, I get it. You've told Ted. No wonder he's so angry. Well, I'm getting the marshmallows."

With the party whirling and spinning around me, Zara's words were spinning too. No wonder he's so angry. That's what I had seen in Ted's face. Anger. Like the heat coming off the fire. In that moment, I realised Ted knew about Billy. Ted must be the one who found Billy in school and tried to attack him. What was it Zara had just said? Ted looked busy.

Ted must be planning to do something to Billy.

I set off to the end of the garden and the hole under the fence.

I had to warn Billy.

Chapter 40
Billy

I sent Callie a message to say thanks for finding the bag and went to the chip shop. There were loads of fireworks going off, and the sound of bangs and screaming rockets. When we still had Dad, we used to go to one of those big displays you pay for.

I ate my fish and chips and looked out at the splashes of orange in the night sky. Soon I would be back at Callie's in the summerhouse. It was good in there. And only one more night to go; tomorrow evening Mum would be home.

I made my way back to school and sneaked in while the cleaners were leaving.

I checked the time. Nearly seven. I don't know why Callie would ask to meet me to hand over the bag. Did she need to tell me something? Maybe she wanted to warn me that her mum and dad's party would end late.

I didn't mind, as long as my bag was safely back with me.

I crawled out of our classroom window and saw Callie coming towards me. She must have come under the fence. But she wasn't carrying my bag. She wasn't looking at me at all. She was looking behind me at the new classrooms and the scaffolding.

I turned. Something was moving on the scaffolding. The lights on the top cast a glow, like street lamps, so I could see a person climbing, all dressed in black.

The scaffolding was made of metal poles bolted together with planks as platforms and walkways. There were no ladders. This person was small, springing around, pulling themselves up like a gymnast, swinging out across a gap. On the ground, a second figure flopped about. I gasped. No. Not another real person – a stuffed figure wearing something striped red and white.

I began to run. Callie hadn't sent that message about my bag. This person had taken my hoodie and dressed some stupid giant doll in it and it lay on the ground beside the torn tarpaulin. I realised who the climber was too. I couldn't see his face, but I recognised him now, and lots of things became clear in my head.

It was Ted.

Chapter 41
Callie

I watched, astonished.

Ted climbed like a professional climber, his hands reaching up, grasping the metal poles of the scaffolding, his feet feeling for the next level. The building was higher than a house and he had somehow managed to already reach the first-floor rooms. He pulled himself up on the planks and looked around. A rope was coiled over one shoulder, spooling out from something lying on the ground – a bulky object like a huge fish on a line, flopping around. What was that? My thoughts whirled. What had Ted done?

"Ted! Come down!" I shouted.

But then, across the playground, Billy appeared from our classroom window. He set off towards me, saw my face and turned, noticing the bulky object on the ground and Ted scurrying along and up the scaffolding. For a whole shocked moment, we both watched Ted leaping, then Billy set off, running over there.

But he wasn't quick enough to stop what Ted did next. Near the top, Ted pulled on his rope and the object rose and swung away, just missing Billy's outstretched arms, bouncing off the metal towers. Now I could see it was a stuffed figure, dressed in Billy's special hoodie.

"No!" Billy shouted, and began to climb after it.

"Billy!" I shouted. "Don't!" But I was already running over there too.

Billy stumbled along the lower planks, reached up and tried to pull himself up on to the next level, but dropped down again cursing. He was the opposite kind of climber to Ted. He tried again, slipping and sliding, losing his grip and falling. He wasn't tall enough to reach the poles on the next level or strong enough to hang on, and he lost his foothold over and over.

No one teaches you how to climb scaffolding. He did a huge leap and swing, crashing into the poles, hung there, got a knee up on to the planks and finally clambered up on to the level above.

"Stop. Both of you. Stop!" I shouted.

I pulled out my phone and messaged Zara. Come to school NOW. Tell parents.

I looked up and gulped. The scaffolding towers seemed to sway. Panic rose inside me. I can't stand high places. I remembered the waterfall we visited on holiday and the steep climb up one side of it, everyone else overtaking me. My legs had turned to jelly on the slope. I remember gripping Dad's arm and pleading, "I can't do it. I just can't," and painfully retracing my steps down while everyone else carried on up.

"Come down!" I screamed.

Maybe there was something else I could do to help.

Get something soft for them to fall on?

I pelted round to the recycling bins and found some old mats from gym lessons. I pulled one out, dragged it under the scaffolding and ran back for another. There was loads of stuff round there – packaging from the new windows, coils of plastic, extra planks.

I ran back.

The stuffed figure was being winched high above Billy. He'd never get to it.

From his place on the highest scaffolding boards, Ted reached out, pulled the stuffed body towards him and dragged it along to the peak of the roof. There, he propped it on a pole like a figurehead on the front of a ship. I could see the strange dummy – the chest pillowy and fat, padded arms sticking out, an awful grinning cheery face. And dressed up in Billy's special hoodie.

Ted held up what looked like sticks. I gasped.

"No!" Billy cried out, in a desperate howl from below him. "Give it back!"

"Don't, Ted!" I shouted.

Trailing strands flickered. There was a flash of bright light. Fire licked around the stuffed figure, turning it into a flaming torch.

I screamed, "Stop!"

The stuffed figure caught fire in a blaze of orange and red. Ted whooped, jumping around on the boards. He was celebrating.

Then he set off down, leaving the blazing dummy lighting up the sky.

Halfway up the building, Billy tried to leap a gap but he stumbled, catching a pole with one hand but losing his grip and pitching forward. His arms flailed, his legs bicycled and he flipped upside down.

"Argh!" he screamed.

He dropped forward then jolted to a stop; the belt on his trousers had hooked itself over a sticking-out scaffolding pole. He hung there, stuck.

"Callie! Do something! Help me!" he shouted.

He was stuck. He couldn't turn. If he undid his belt, he would fall like a stone.

Panic filled me and I managed to drag myself up on to the first level of scaffolding. The poles were cool, with sharp edges. I scrabbled to climb. Billy was miles above me. I stumbled and fell, hitting my knee on the side of a pole. "OW! OW!"

How would I climb that far? My stomach lurched. This was straight up. I would never get all the way to where Billy was. Not in a million years.

But he couldn't climb down. He couldn't get anywhere. And if I couldn't help him, the belt could break. His trousers could tear. He was bound to fall...

"Help!" I screamed.

Below me, Ted reached the ground.

It was no use. I hoisted myself down, stumbled back towards him and looked up to where Billy hung, like an astronaut floating in space. A scream was coming from him. A thin, terrible, dragging scream of pain and terror. It cut right through me. "Ted! Look at him!" I shouted. "He's stuck. You have to go back up and help him!"

And now my eyes were drawn to the blazing stuffed figure on the top of the building. It had caught fire like a rocket, and now it had dissolved and was coming apart. Sparks and chunks drifted, dancing down and landing all over the playground. Some fell in the recycling bin. There was a wuff sound as sparks set the contents on fire, and then a roar. Flames leapt high out of the bin. Billy's terrified scream rose over the roar.

When those scaffolding planks caught fire…

Ted stared at me. His face had a distant look.

"Do something!" I screamed. "Go back. He'll fall! You're the only one who can help him!"

One of the panels leaning near the bin caught fire. Flames shot up and licked the side of the scaffolding.

The whole side of the building glowed and sparked.

"Help him!"

Ted seemed to decide. In a bound, he ran back towards school and vaulted back on to the scaffolding. He was at the opposite end to the fire. He'd take a while to get to Billy. He was fast but … the flames!

I had to help. Had to stop the fire … slow it down.

I ran round behind the recycling and began

pulling piles of packaging away from the bin and the flames, hurling them near the gates. I was coughing. I pulled the cuffs of my fleece over my hands, ran to the bin and whacked at the flames to smother them. I threw part of a mat on top of the bin. I panted and whacked. My eyes stung with smoke. A wall of heat rose in front of me. The fire was winning. Explosions sounded.

I couldn't see what I was doing any more and I staggered around coughing. Sharp pain zigzagged across my hands. The side of a mat was sticking to me and I flung it off. Pain like knives shot across my hand and wrist. Everywhere seemed to be heat and jagged orange flames.

My head spun. Someone was shouting. Figures were running across the playground, lit up in the dizzy bright sparks.

I found myself staggering back out across the playground, gulping air.

And then I looked up at the new classrooms and saw that Ted had reached a place just below Billy on the scaffolding. Billy kicked out wildly.

"Ted's trying to help you!" I shouted, but my voice wasn't there any more and I seemed to be swaying. I couldn't feel my hands.

Ted swung himself out, reaching for Billy's legs. Maybe he could pull him in. But Billy kicked him away. Ted caught a leg and held on. Next thing, Ted had Billy round the waist and he was scrabbling to keep his balance.

But then they both seemed to tip. I heard a cry.

Two dark shapes, locked together, fell.

They landed with a thud.

Voices. Rushing people. Billy groaning, sprawled across the mat. Ted curled up nearby.

I couldn't think properly.

I wanted to get to them but my legs wouldn't work. I sank down.

Someone called, "Don't move them. Quick. Call an ambulance."

Chapter 42
Billy

I woke up. White walls. A smell of cleaning. Glassy bright light. Faraway voices. Hospital.

Everything hurt.

I tried moving my legs, but pain shot down them.

Which bits of me were broken? My arm was very heavy and when I tried to lift it there was a plaster cast on it and pain was stabbing all the way down. A broken arm.

I turned my head. A beaker of water. A box of tissues. Another bed. And in it, Ted with a big bandage round his head.

My heart did a major flip. Was this a dream? Panic filled me. How long had we been lying here? Why would they put us next to each other? Where were the nurses?

Help! Ted was dangerous. He was crackers. My head spun. But I couldn't keep my eyes open. I was floating. My arm twinged like someone was digging inside it.

Some time later, I woke again. The world still seemed hazy.

I tried to sit up but too many bits of me wouldn't let me. As I slowly turned my head to check, there was Ted, still lying in the bed on the other side of me.

His eyes were shut. The bandage made his head look enormous. But suddenly his eyes blinked open. He saw me. "Not talking to you," he groaned.

"Ow!" I said, trying to push myself on to one elbow.

"I hope your arm falls off," Ted said.

I was furious. "It's your fault. You just burned all my things. And it was you in the library ... those messages. You're weird."

"You're worse," he said.

"Shut up."

"No, you shut up."

"Make me."

"You're rubbish at climbing," Ted murmured. And then, "Why did you climb up?"

"I wanted my hoodie."

"The red one?"

"Yeah. You destroyed it." I wanted to wipe my eyes, but my arm came up and it was the broken one and I sort of whacked myself on the side of the head with it. "Ow!"

No one said anything after that. My arm twanged. I must have fallen asleep again.

Chapter 43

Ted

I lay silent in a hospital bed. Someone was in the bed next to me and I turned to look. Billy. I blinked. Still Billy. And again. Still Billy. The world spun and then it went still. I let my mind drift.

A voice woke me. Mum had arrived. Her voice crowded in, loud and demanding. "What's happened? I got a message to come. They said you fell." She rushed around me like a busy bird, checking the bandage on my head, pushing where it was taped. "The doctor says you've got concussion. From the fall." She patted my hand. "They said you fell from some scaffolding you'd been climbing. I told them you would never do that. You must have got the wrong boy. That was not my Ted. It's not true, is it?"

The silence filled up.

Mum's face opened in a gasp. "Ted?"

I closed my eyes again.

"Why, Ted? Why would you do that?"

I sighed. The words seemed heavy and my mouth was stuffed with dry twigs. "I had … to get him back." It took a long time to say. Mum looked at me intently. I swallowed. "Billy … from the class assembly. I stole his hoodie and set it on fire."

Mum clutched him. "What? Oh Ted! Is he OK? Did he fall off too?"

"He's behind you."

With a little cry, Mum turned and stared at the next bed. Billy's eyes were shut. "Ted, what have you done to him?"

"He took my friend away. And he made me look stupid."

"That's not a good enough reason. You could both have died."

"I would never have died. I can climb really well."

She stared at me in amazement. "Can you?"

"He's a rubbish climber. And he got stuck. Sort of hooked on. I was trying to help him but he wouldn't let me. I could have saved both of us."

Mum stood up. "Ted, the doctor wants to see me. I'm going to leave you for a while. I'll come back."

I watched her go and wished I was far away.

Chapter 44

Billy

I listened to Ted and his mum talking.

He said he was trying to help me when he climbed back up. I tried to remember. Was that what happened?

There was a belt on those trousers I found in Lost Property. They were too big. That's right. They were good but they weren't my size. I'd got hooked by the belt.

He'd climbed back up… Yes. And he'd reached up.

That was true.

I thought he was trying to attack me but … why would he bother? He must have known I was going to fall.

So he climbed up again to … try to help me?

My thoughts went blurry. Someone came running down the ward to my bed. Mum. She was pulling her wheelie case. She must have just got off the plane.

"Billy!" She swept me in a hug and dragged my arm into the hug too. "I've missed you!"

"Ow!" I yelped. "Ow, ow!"

Mum smelled of apple shampoo and holidays.

"Is it just the arm?" She looked at the charts at the end of my bed. "Bruising. No concussion."

She was using her nurse voice. "Just your arm broken. What have you been doing? Poor thing. They said you climbed up a building. Did you?" She pulled back the bedding and checked my legs. "Can you feel this? That's just a bruise. Have you got pain anywhere else, love?"

"Most of me," I said.

"I'm not surprised!" She sat down beside me on the bed. "Spill the beans then. What's been going on?"

"It was a sort of ... argument. Ted had my hoodie. That United one."

"Where did he get that?"

"I brought it with me, in my overnight bag."

"What, and you climbed up to get it back? Oh, Billy." She hugged me again.

"Ow! You're squeezing me. Don't squeeze me, Mum."

"I've got to squeeze you. I've missed a whole week!"

"Did you have a good holiday, Mum?"

"So." Mum stopped speaking. "I'm going to talk to the nurses about you. And then I'll come back."

Mum was home. I would be going back home to my bedroom. She'd had her holiday. I closed my eyes and drifted off.

I felt her hand on my forehead again and opened my eyes. "You're going to be fine. They've X-rayed your legs. It's just the arm. You've had a lucky escape."

Mum looked different; new and sparkly. I grinned at her.

"Here you are!" said a deep voice. Someone else was standing at the end of my bed. Dad. Mum and Dad. At the same time. Nuclear explosion!

Dad dumped a carrier bag on the bed. "I got you these, from the shop," he said. "Heard about the … accident."

Mum turned on him. "Why wasn't Billy with you last night?"

Dad looked like he wanted to turn round and run out again. He pushed his hand through his hair as if he was going to pull it out. "Look," he said. "I took a job. Billy was fine to stay at the house, weren't you, Billy? But he went to a friend's, didn't you?"

"You went to a friend's? How come?" Mum asked. Her voice was firm. No messing.

"Patti told me you were doing a project," Dad said.

"What project? Where was it you went, Billy?" Mum asked.

She was on the warpath. She wasn't going to stop. I wanted to be swallowed up in the bed or, better still, find another universe.

From beside us came Ted's voice. "Billy was in school."

"What?" Mum and Dad both looked round at Ted.

They turned back to me. "Come on, Billy, what's been going on?" Mum said. And then, to Dad, "You told me you'd be at home all week."

Dad threw his hands in the air. "I got offered some work. We talked about it. Billy knew all about it, didn't you, mate?"

Ted's voice came again. "He slept in school."

Mum and Dad sort of reared back then turned on me. "What! Billy, you didn't?"

"Not every night," I said. "I stayed at Callie's."

"Who's Callie?" Mum and Dad both said.

"She lives near school," Ted said.

They turned to look at him again. "Who are you?"

"I'm Ted," he said.

I interrupted then. I might as well tell them

everything. "Dad, it was Kingsley. She said I couldn't stay," I said. "She made it clear."

"Kingsley?" Dad's face changed. He breathed in loudly. "Oh, Billy, I'm so sorry."

"How could you?" Mum shrieked. "I trusted you."

"Don't argue!" I said loudly. "Please."

Mum and Dad went quiet. Mum's face looked like a kettle about to boil but she stroked my fingers.

"I'm so sorry, love. Why didn't you tell me?"

"I wanted you to have your holiday."

Dad's face filled up with misery.

"Kingsley hates me, Dad," I said.

He put his hand to his mouth. "Oh no." He shook his head. "Billy, I think you'll find it's me she hates. She's been pretty ... explosive, since the baby. If I'd thought for a minute she'd pick on you... I'm so sorry, mate."

"So I couldn't stay at your house," I said.

"I can't believe it," Mum said. "You slept in the school?" Her voice was small and sad. "Oh, love!"

"I'll talk to Kingsley," Dad said.

Mum stroked my hair.

Dad came right beside me. "I'm so sorry. I hear

your hoodie got burned."

I felt tears coming then. I couldn't stop myself. "I'd rather have you, Dad," I said.

Dad's mouth wobbled and shook.

Mum just sat there on the other side of me, staring at Dad in a flat, cold, dead way.

He wriggled about like a fish on a hook. "I'll look out for another hoodie. They do the raffles every year so there's every chance..."

I didn't know if that was true. My arm hurt. I wondered if Dad really would try. But he'd started speaking again. "Um. Look, Billy, I'll see you soon. I'll drop by again. You'll be out of hospital before you know it." He did one of his beaming smiles. He patted the plaster on my arm. He leapt back up and did a thumbs-up. "OK, you take care now. I'm glad you're OK, mate."

Mum stayed a bit longer. She kept smoothing the bed and asking if I needed things, then she got up. "I'll be back to check on you in the morning," she said.

She hadn't unpacked from the holiday yet. She'd got a call to come straight here.

It felt very quiet after she had gone.

Chapter 45

Callie

Dad came to the hospital with me.

We had kept my hands wrapped up in wet tea towels and it was horrible when they peeled them off but the doctors said we had done just the right thing. That was Mum. She knows loads of first aid.

First we saw the doctor in the clinic. The burns weren't as deep as they first thought. They would heal without having skin grafts. My palms were the worst. They were seeping and puffy. Just leave those blisters alone, they said. Then they put lots of creams on them to help them heal and stop infections, and bandaged them up. You've been lucky, they kept saying.

While we waited by the pharmacy, I asked if we could go and see Ted and Billy.

"I'm not sure," Dad said.

"I just want to see they are all right. Please, Dad?"

"Just for a few minutes," he said.

Ted and Billy were in beds next to each other. Ted had a bandage round his head and was lying propped up on pillows. Billy's arm was in a sling and he was sitting up. They had empty beds on both sides of them.

"Callie!" Ted said.

"Oh, hi, Callie," said Billy.

There was someone hoovering in the corridor. We all stared at each other.

The noise stopped and the room went quiet.

"Your hands," Ted said. "What happened to your hands, Callie?"

"They got burned."

I nearly said, What did you expect?!

Ted's mouth opened in a wide shocked expression. He shook his head. "Are they sore?"

"What do you think?"

The words came out loud and cross. What a stupid question. "I've just been to see the doctors," I said.

"Oh no." Ted's mouth sort of crumbled. "Callie, I'm sorry. I'm really sorry your hands got hurt."

We were quiet again.

"What about you?" I asked.

"Concussion. I have to stay lying down," Ted said.

Billy waved his arm. "Broken," he said. "In two places."

It was weird seeing them next to each other. Last time I'd seen them they'd been hanging from the scaffolding in the dark and falling off. Now they were wearing those weird white and blue hospital nightshirts.

I had wanted to see them but now I felt so odd being here with both of them in the bright ward.

"I hope you get better," I said, which is a stupid thing to say in a hospital, because everyone hopes everyone will get better. That's what hospitals are for.

As Dad and I walked back down the ward, I thought about how Ted had said sorry about my hands. Mum and Dad always make us say sorry. When Chloe and Ollie fight, we all have to talk about it and say sorry before anything can carry on in life.

When I told Mum and Dad everything that had happened, they had asked lots of questions and I know they would have made Ted and Billy say sorry to each other before they would ever let them get out of those beds.

Sorry means you care about a person. Sorry means you might have been wrong. Sorry shows you feel bad. That's why I always hate it when they make me say it. But when my brother and sister get forced to say it to me, it's like the tide coming in and washing away some of the bad feelings.

Chapter 46
Billy

The evening came and we had hospital meals. I dropped my fork into the bed and I couldn't get the top off the yoghurt.

Callie must be messing up everything eating her dinner; she had bandages on both hands.

She'd been trying to stop the fire from reaching the scaffolding. From reaching me. If she hadn't done that…

It got dark. The hospital smelled like medicine. I was very bored and the nurses bought some books but they were for really little kids.

I lay in the silence and my arm throbbed.

"Ted, are you awake?" I asked into the silence.

"No," came Ted's reply.

"Ted… Did the orange juice come out?"

No reply.

"There's lots of spare trousers in Lost Property. We could find some for you?"

Silence.

"How come you can climb like that? How did you get to the top?"

"I learned it."

"How, though?"

"I don't know."

Silence again.

"Why did you do it? Why did you take my hoodie?"

Ted sighed. Then, suddenly, he said, "What's Kingsley like?"

"Her! She basically hates my guts."

"Do you pretend she's a troll?"

"I tried it but she's worse than a troll."

"Oh."

Some time went by.

Ted's voice again. "Where did you get your hoodie?"

"My dad got it after a Cup game. They raffled it. It was first prize, signed by the players."

"Yeah, I saw the signatures. We could ask Callie to look. There might be some bits. They might have fallen in the playground and not got burned."

"I don't think there'd be any bits. It was all gone."

We were quiet then.

I had an idea. I felt around on my bed. "My dad brought me these sweets," I said. "My arm... I can't get the wrappers off. In the morning... I just thought ... maybe..."

Chapter 47
Callie

When I called in to visit Ted and Billy the next day, Billy was sitting on Ted's bed. Ted's head was still bandaged. Billy's arm was still in plaster. But the big thing was, when they both looked up at me, their faces were … friendly.

"Callie!" they called.

Each of them had a pile of sweets. Ted was unwrapping them, one for him, one for Billy. He held out one to me.

I threw my bandaged hands in the air. "Look… I can't…"

"How about I unwrap the sweets and throw them in your mouth," Billy said. "Like dogs."

I smiled then, even though he still made me cross. "It's OK. I don't want a sweet."

I looked at Ted, then across at Billy, then at Ted again. "You're talking to each other."

They grinned. "Yep."

Billy and Ted's must be the most unlikeliest friendship in the history of the world.

In the weeks afterwards, we were in massive disgrace, of course: Billy got de-prefected and Ted got suspended from school for a week. Now he has to go and talk to a school counsellor. We all got in huge trouble for going inside the playground and into school. The police interviewed Billy and Ted and then all of us as a group. Zara cried and Nico said stuff about his human rights and the confiscated skateboard until the policeman said, "I think we've heard enough from you," and then he shut up. Mum and Dad kept saying I had let them down and "We know you were trying to help Billy but what you did was dangerous and you should have come and told us what was going on." I couldn't play netball. I missed two big matches and even when the bandages came off, my palms were still blistered and sore.

The fire had caused damage to the school. Mrs Alexander talked about it in an assembly. Dad said the builders shouldn't have left so many materials leaned up against the new classrooms. It wasn't all our fault. We watched the builders cleaning and repairing the walls. We were in disgrace, really. We couldn't be trusted. We'd let everyone down.

The hole under my fence got filled in so no one could ever do such a stupid thing again. We all stood and watched from my garden while Mr Rafferty brought a wheelbarrow full of cement and a shovel. It felt like a ceremony. All of us stood quiet and still, even the little ones that Mum childminds, who are never quiet.

"Those badgers are little..." Mr Rafferty swore under his breath, and we all laughed, and then it was over.

Chapter 48

Billy

The plaster's coming off my arm soon. It really stinks. I can't play football yet. I've been to watch two matches with Dad. He says he'll come to my training more often, when they let me play again. He told me Kingsley's sorry for what she did. Patti had a major go at her, he said. Mum's back working at the hospital.

At school they said, "Well, Billy, we don't think you are quite right for a prefect at the moment," and they took the badge away. I asked Mr Rafferty if I could help him and he said, "Don't be stupid, how can you be any help with a broken arm?"

Next day Ted came with me and we tried again, knocking on the door of his workroom next to the library.

"You two?" Mr Rafferty said.

"We wondered if you needed anything sorting or labelling in your office?"

They've made us Caretaker Cupboard Monitors. We're sorting all the tools. Mrs Alexander said, "It's a responsible job, Billy. And you, Ted."

And I said, "It's OK, we'll ace it."

"I'm sure you will," she said. "Let's see how it goes."

After one of the matches, I went back to Dad's.

I actually held the baby, until she did a poo. She's all right. I mean, she can't talk yet but she's stopped screaming. Poppy, she's called. Dad said she's going to love playing with her big brother when she's older. She's lucky, she gets to be part of two families. Except she has to have Kingsley as her big sister. I'll warn her about that.

Chapter 49

Callie

I don't think they'll ever pick me as a prefect, after what happened. Dad says I can be the dishwasher prefect for the rest of my life, if that helps.

Our teacher Mr Dunlop is still grumpy. But the difference is, when he comes out with something like, "Well, I am disappointed, Elm Class. Standards of behaviour have dropped," and rubs his ear with the back of his hand, Billy's eyes gleam and we all perk up and say Classic troll behaviour under our breath. The entire class joins in. And Dunlop looks around, so puzzled and cross. He honestly has no idea who started it!

Chapter 50

Ted

Once I was back, after being suspended from school, I showed the others all the places where the badger dug. I even pretended to be one, wiggling my bum and pawing the ground. They all laughed but I didn't mind. They said they couldn't believe about my climbing. We all went into my garden and I showed them how I do it. I climbed up my tree really fast, the way I always do, and sat high up in my hollow.

"Whoa!" they all said.

Callie said, "I'm not brave enough to climb up that high," and laughed. Nico didn't get very high either, just panicked and jumped down.

Ted's the brave one. They said that.

Billy wants us both to go bouldering at a climbing wall where you learn all the grips and techniques. His arm's not strong enough yet but it will be soon.

Now I'm going to Callie's house three days a week. I go round there after tea. Mum discussed it with Callie's mum, and she offered. It's not a childminding thing. I'm helping with the little ones.

Callie walks to school with me and we chat. We often meet at break and lunchtimes, sitting on the planter by the football pitch, or I help Billy in the caretaker cupboard. Mum is still very busy with work and at weekends I'm learning to make the dinner. We've bought bikes. Sometimes at night, when Mum is asleep, I climb up and sit in my hollow, surrounded by leaves, and look out on the garden next door, the summerhouse and the tyre. And then across the fence at my school in darkness. Sometimes I even get to see the badger.

I suppose I will always be a watcher. But that's OK.

Chapter 51

Callie

I used to think I could sort out my friends when life got tricky but it turns out you can't always help people, even if you want to. Life doesn't work out like that. But we are all back together. We even decided on a group name: The Insiders. It was Ted's idea. I love it.

Acknowledgements

Bullying is never just a single event; it ripples out and damages us all.

Huge thanks for ideas and input: my writers' group, Julian, Kryss, Lesley and Alison, the Briggses, the Howes.

Thanks also to my brilliant agent Anne Clark and my inspiring editor Tom Bonnick, who always knows where the story needs to go.